ALLEGRA MAUD GOLDMAN

ALLEGRA MAUD GOLDMAN

Edith Konecky

Foreword by Alix Kates Shulman

Introduction by Tillie Olsen

Afterword by Bella Brodzki

THE FEMINIST PRESS
AT THE CITY UNIVERSITY OF NEW YORK
NEW YORK

Published by The Feminist Press at The City University of New York
The Graduate Center, 365 Fifth Avenue, Suite 5406, New York, NY 10016
www.feministpress.org.

Second Feminist Press edition, 2001

Library of Congress Cataloging-in-Publication Data

Konecky, Edith.
    Allegra Maud Goldman / Edith Konecky ; introduction by Tillie Olsen ; after-
word by Bella Brodzki.
        p. cm.
    ISBN 1-55861-281-5 (pbk. : alk. paper)
    1. Brooklyn (New York, N.Y.)—Fiction. 2. Jewish families—Fiction. 3. Jewish
girls—Fiction. I. Title.

PS3561.O457 A79 2001
813'.54—dc21

                                                                2001040639

The Feminist Press would like to thank Mariam K. Chamberlain, Florence Howe,
Joanne Markell, and Genevieve Vaughan for their generosity in supporting this publication.

Cover design by Dayna Navaro
Cover photo courtesy of Edith Konecky
Original text design by Sidney Feinberg

Printed in the United States of America on acid-free paper by McNaughton & Gunn.

05 04 03 02 01   6 5 4 3 2 1

*This book is dedicated to my parents,
Harry and Elizabeth Rubin; to the MacDowell Colony,
where much of it was written; and to whoever that was,
real or imagined, quiet in the corner, waiting for pages.*

Then there *is* something I
can do I
can find your name for you
that's the key to everything once you'd
repeat it clearly you'd
get up and walk knowing where you're
going where you
came from

The Key to Everything
M AY S WENSON

Foreword

Allegra Maud Goldman is one of those rare delights, a novel of
childhood (in this case, growing up well-to-do and misunderstood in Jewish Depression-era Brooklyn) that is as wise and
true as it is funny.

The story opens with Allegra at three in a typical rebellious
act: conning a cop into getting her an ice-cream cone after she
has shaken her father at Coney Island. From then on we follow
along as this smart little girl makes the important discoveries
en route to puberty. She takes us through the familiar rites of
middle-class Jewish childhood: dancing lessons, Dick-and-Jane
readers, summer resort and summer camp, synagogue and
cemetery. Fortunately Allegra is precocious: fortunately for her
because she needs all her wits and spunk to make sense out of
a preposterous world; fortunately for us because we get to
watch her cunning encounters with family, teachers, friends.

Her family: a self-made garment-manufacturing father ("If he
had to make himself . . . why couldn't he have made himself
nicer?") who, despite "a corner house with three bathrooms
and a Buick and a chauffeur and a cook," can think of nothing
but saving pennies. A card- and Mah-Jongg-playing mother
who, between phone calls and golf dates, darns socks as a
defense against her husband's "occasional accusations that she

wasn't holding up her end." A brother, David, whose attachment to the piano is so subversive of the family's plans for him that they hire a psychiatrist to cure him of it. Kitchen-haunting Jewish grandmothers, bureaucratic teachers, belligerent playmates, primping cousins, idolized camp counselors. Most of the expected types are here in short set chapters, crisply rendered by Konecky's wit like *gribbenes* from chicken fat; yet they are observed with such fresh or salty affection that one seems to be encountering them for the first time. Not only are there rich sketches of major characters, but a dress salesman and school principal are deftly rendered in perfect satirical one-liners.

Besides these often hilarious takes, Konecky gives us an inner portrait of Allegra, a lovable brat coming honestly, even painfully, out of the fog of family through the trials of childhood into adult knowledge. (Perhaps "brat" is simply a put-down for a certain sort of independent child, as "bitch" is a put-down for a kind of independent woman.) We watch Allegra uncover the facts of life and the facts of death with tough determination. She grapples with pneumonia and the body, religion and the soul. She learns that people live differently, that "money was not the most important thing in the world," that death gets everyone.

As her father avoided his elders' plans for him and her grandparents escaped their parents' plans for them, Allegra faces down the unacceptable expectations adults keep setting for her. Though her parents ignore Allegra's need to "find herself" in favor of son David's (" 'Oh, you,' my mother said. 'You'll grow up and marry some nice man and have children. David is a boy' "), Allegra the emerging writer seduces her father into giving her a typewriter by letting him imagine her a secretary. Similarly, at school she confronts the principal with the absurdity of "home ec" classes for girls ("I came to school to improve my mind, not to learn toast and applesauce") and shop for boys ("All the boys around here are planning to be gynecologists or ear, nose, and throat men. How come you're preparing them to be carpenters?"). Slowly her narrow world expands through books, friends, and experience until by the end of the novel a "person" has emerged. By then, at thirteen, Allegra knows enough of life to fashion a true and complex poem—an independent act that brings publication, ten dollars, and with them even her father's dim respect. Now it is clear that Allegra will no longer be "doomed to that house, those parents, my brother, this street, this borough" as she once had been; now her center is "in her own heart."

There is probably something for everybody in this short, funny book that had me laughing and crying to the last page. Even today's "young adults" will recognize, alas, too much. My daughter read the book when she was fourteen and loved it as much as I, though predictably her favorite scene is set in school while mine, which I found even funnier the second time round, occurs at the father's "place of business."

As frequently happens in books about childhood, Allegra occasionally seems to know a bit more about her situation than any child, however precocious, can know—particularly, more about sexism than such a child could have known back then. But surely this is a minor quibble with a story that, even twenty-five years after its first happy publication, comes across as overwhelmingly, convincingly, enduringly true.

Alix Kates Shulman

Introduction

That *Allegra Maud Goldman!*

Twent-five years ago, in all her morning freshness, she metamorphosed right up off the printed page, her created world floating about her, and without a by-your-leave took up full-being'd permanent residence in my mind and heart, insinuating into my vision, my stance.

And not only into mine. I thrust her on my writer friends, my true reader friends, my daughters of various ages. For all of us she became a common reference. (O yes, we say: Just like Allegra. . . . Or, Remember when Allegra . . . ? Or, As Allegra observed . . .)

And then, one by one, the young daughters of my friends, and granddaughters, stole our *Allegras* to circulate among enchanted peers. For whom she became a source of self-knowledge and sustainment and common reference. And shrieks of merriment.

They did not need to steal her. All along she was, is, and rightfully so, in my library's Junior Classics section—

Allegra is *my* age, my friends'—and daughters'—and granddaughters'—age, an *any*-age Classic—one of the few books that proves to be a timeless delight for all ages.

Allegra?

On the surface so seemingly, well, light. Charm, of course. Wit on every page. ("I have a terrible memory. I never forget a thing.") Deft story telling, skating us right along on the surface with seemingly effortless grace. Familiar territory—the limited, limiting, and material-minded Jewish family, the well-to-do neighborhood, the school. And transcending it all the precocious misunderstood young one with an undeceived eye. Familiar. Light. Surface.

That is the legerdemain. Before we come to realize it, it is *not* easy, familiar, light, at all. The shadows, the depths, surround. We are seized, drawn into full dimension justness, "The heart of the matter." And, as in life, all braided with laughter.

Allegra—child, girl—*is* a marvel of creation, firmly set in her particularity, her fifty-year-ago, pre-bas-mitzvah, pre-Jewish Feminism, pre-having-a-destiny-other-than-marriage, time. Alone, she has to discover about being female; about sex; about being trapped in a human body that someday must die—and how to come to terms with these. Alone, she has to try to reconcile the narrowness, bigotries, limitations of her family as she comes to recognize them—with her love for them and their love (in whatever form) given to her.

Allegra, "breaking the thick walls of self," sees others not only as they affect her, but tries to explain, understand them; tries also to discover, cling to, the truth of what she has experienced—separated from what her world insists has worth; is the meaning, content, of her experiencings.

Allegra lives solidly in her senses, her heart, her burgeoning intellect. She comes to us in all her ferocious realism, her devastating and constantly practiced powers of observation and reflection: her perspicacity. Always, she is concerned with "the getting of wisdom," the search for what is truly one's own, and the cleaving to it. She is truly one of the rare and precious portraits of the artist as a young girl.

No wonder that sentient, pre-pubescent girls, treading their own perilous way forty, fifty years later, delight in her, cherish her.

In other hands, only Allegra would have been accorded respect, development, possibility—let alone the best lines. In other hands—as is and has been too often the case—that first generation able to live beyond the age-old imperative of survival—in this instance Allegra's Jewish family—would have been pilloried, or satirized, or scanted; used for ridicule, or at best for laughs.

But they live with us in fullest human dimension. Through Edith Konecky's wise, encompassing comprehensions we recognize the universality of their strugglings, errings, strengths; the forces that shape, motivate. In the best Chekhovian sense, we are led to know them not only as they are but also as they might have been in other circumstances. We have been reminded, reaffirmed in the truth of human potentiality, the Allegras that never came to be, the Allegras to come.

All this in only 174 pages; in a limited setting; with a deft, light touch; written entirely through the developing perceptions of a child, a young girl (breathtaking technical achievement).

I have used the word "legerdemain." But this is the magic of art—the concealed art of Edith Konecky. Long and multiplied life to *Allegra*.

Tillie Olsen

ALLEGRA MAUD GOLDMAN

Chapter 1

"It's a girl."

In the beginning is the sex. First the entity, it, but only as a bridge to the sex; girl, she. Me. A little later, that particular combination of sounds and symbols, the label, to which it would have to answer, and by which be known.

What could they have been thinking, naming me Allegra? I entered screaming and I'll go out likewise.

Allegra Maud Goldman. There's a whole plot in that name. The heaviness, the richness, the Jewishness of the last name. The dowdiness, the patrician, chilblained Englishness in the middle. And then Allegra! I knew from the beginning that I would never fit that name.

I almost never smile and when I do, I do it slowly.

"What's your name, little girl?"

This is a big pink and blue policeman talking down at me on the boardwalk at Coney Island. Half an hour earlier it came to me that I wasn't getting on too well with my parents and, as there were plenty of other people about, I'd gone off to look for a new set. I was nearly a yardstick high and my heart was full of hope, but in all that time no one had paid the slightest attention to me, much less made a move to adopt me, and my original father had vanished and I was beginning to worry. In fact, I was bawling.

"Are you lost?"

It hadn't occurred to me that I was lost.

"I'm on the boardwalk at Coney Island," I said.

"Where are your mother and daddy?" the cop said.

"I don't know."

"Then you're lost."

I bawled harder.

"What's your name, little girl?"

It took me a minute to remember. *"Allegramaudgoldman,"* I howled.

"What?"

"I want an ice cream cone."

He picked me up and walked me to a stand where he bought me an ice cream cone. Pistachio, his choice. I stopped bawling.

That was the high point of my childhood.

He told me his name was Joe and we were going back to his office and pretty soon my mommy and daddy would come and get me. He carried me to the station house and by the time we got there I had dripped a lot of green ice cream onto his shoulder, but he didn't seem to mind. It was warm in the station house and I was glad to be there. It was around Christmastime. My father liked to take brisk walks in the sea air, no matter what time of year. I hated brisk walks at any time in any kind of air and still do. With my father walking briskly, I had to canter to keep up. We did this almost every Sunday. But that Sunday I decided to hell with it and cantered in the opposite direction. I don't know how long it took him to notice that I wasn't there.

"Now, what's your name, honey. Say it slow."

"Al-le-gra Ma-a-aud Go-o-old–ma-a-an," I said.

"Hey, Mac," he said, turning to a cop who was sitting behind a big, tall desk. "Can you understand this kid?"

The phone rang and Mac picked it up and said yes, they'd just brought in a little girl and yes, she was wearing a navy blue coat and maryjanes and no hat and no, she wasn't crying, and what was that name again?

"Are you going to arrest me?" I said when he'd hung up. He and Joe laughed. They were jolly men. I was disappointed.

"I have to go to the bathroom."

A big lady cop came and took me to the bathroom, which was none too clean.

"You have to put paper on it," I said.

"On what?" she boomed.

"The toilet seat." One thing my mother had drilled into me that I knew absolutely by heart: if you sat on a public, or strange, toilet seat without putting paper on it you got a dread disease. Pressed for further details, she would elaborate, "A social disease."

Social.

When we got back from the bathroom, Arthur was there.

"Is *this* your father?" Joe said, which was stupid, since Arthur was black.

"He's Arthur," I said.

"I'm the chauf*feur*," Arthur said. "Come on, 'Legra."

"This is Joe," I said to Arthur. "He bought me a pistachio ice cream cone. It cost a nickel."

"That's all right," Joe said. "It's on the house."

We took our leave. I got in the back seat and slid the glass partition shut between me and Arthur and unhooked the speaking tube and buzzed Arthur.

"What you want now, 'Legra?" he said. We were tooling nicely down Ocean Parkway.

"I want to steer."

"Ain't you done enough for one day?"

"No."

"Gettin' your ma and pa lathered up like that. Ain't you shamed of yoursef?"

"No."

"Can't steer here. Too much traffic."

"How come you don't tell *me* 'Yes'm'?"

"'Cause you just a little no-'count brat."

"You're fired," I said.

"That the funniest thing I heard all day."

When we got to the corner of our street, he pulled over to the curb and stopped the car.

"Come on up here and steer," he said.

I wriggled through the partition and got on his lap and took the wheel. I couldn't see over it, but I could see between the spokes. I steered all the way down the block, nice and straight, and just before we got to our house, in case anyone was looking, I slid off his lap and Arthur steered us into the driveway.

That's not my earliest recollection. I have a terrible memory; I never forget a thing. Sometimes I think I even remember being born, but maybe that's because I've always been afraid to do anything headfirst, like dive or bellywhop. On the other hand, my mother often accused me of being "headstrong," which sounded like a good thing to me even though she said it as though it were some kind of sin. She said it frequently after the Coney Island episode.

"Allegra got lost," is how she began, as though I were something mindless, like a sock. And then, illogically, "She's so headstrong."

"I did not get lost. I ran away."

How could I explain? How could I explain that I had asked for and been denied the following: a hot dog, a ride on the carousel, a bag of fried potatoes, the Whip, ice cream, to walk barefoot in the sand at the very edge of the surf, Crackerjacks, candy, *anything.* It was "before lunch." It was winter. How could I explain that after all those no's I was even more than usually reluctant to endure the final part of the Sunday morning ritual, which was to sit quietly on a stool at Feltman's watching my father eat two dozen clams (sometimes it was oysters) on the half shell. He would offer me one—he would offer to teach me how to eat it and I, who would later learn to share his enthusiasm, would look at the cold, gray, slimy, unevolved creatures that he assured me were "alive," even as he devoured them, and decline. "Not yet," I would say, holding out hope.

How could you eat anything that was alive, even if it didn't appear to be especially so? Just knowing.

"Flowers are alive," my father said, "and you pick them. Anyhow, it probably dies when it's pulled from the shell." He was at that moment spearing one of the naked little bodies and ripping it from its last stubborn mooring.

This business of life! This business of *being!*

"What are you going to be when you grow up?"

My favorite question. Everyone over a certain height asked it. You'd think the whole world turned on what Allegra Maud Goldman was going to *be* when she grew up. I never gave the same answer twice.

"A gentleman farmer," I said to Mrs. Oxfelder, who was helping me into a blue butterfly dress with big gauze wings. She was about to give me my first dancing lesson.

"Ha, ha," said Mrs. Oxfelder, not unkindly. "You can't be a gentleman farmer, Allegra. You're a girl."

"I'm going to change," I said. A girl was something else I was beginning to learn I might be stuck with, and it was not the best thing to be. I had an older brother, David, and he was something it was better to be. He was a boy. He had a bicycle.

"Wouldn't you like to be a dancer?" Mrs. Oxfelder said. "A lovely, graceful vision, music for the eye, making all the people sigh and dream and weep and cry *bravo?*"

"No."

"Using your body to say all the magical, miracle things music says? And love says?"

"No."

"Perhaps you'll change your mind," she said, leading me by the hand into a large room where I stood shivering among a lot of other butterflies, some of them fat.

"This is Allegra, girls, our newest *danseuse.*" She sat down at the piano and played a few arpeggios. "Now, girls, I am going to play some airy spring music and I want you to listen to it. Then I want you to think of yourselves as lovely butterflies, free and joyous in the beautiful sunlit sky. And remember, the delicious flowers are blooming everywhere."

She played and the girls started to flit about, flapping their arms and sucking on imaginary flowers. I couldn't believe my eyes. I clamped them shut and threw myself onto the floor, where I lay spread-eagled. The music abruptly ceased.

"Allegra! What kind of butterfly is that?"

"A dead one in a glass case in the Museum of Natural History," I muttered.

6

"This is the *dance,*" Mrs. Oxfelder said, her voice shrill. "It is not science. Get up off the floor."

It was a long hour, and when my mother came to get me at the end of it, she was wearing her brave face. Where I was concerned, she was usually filled with forebodings.

"Twinkletoes she's not," Mrs. Oxfelder said, handing me over.

"That's why she's here," my mother said.

On the way home in the car I sulked. "I'm not ever going back there again," I said.

"Yes you are."

"David doesn't have to."

"David is a boy."

"I'll kill myself," I said. "I don't see why I have to be some crummy bug."

"You're learning to dance."

"The main thing I'm not going to be when I grow up," I said, "is a dancer."

"You have to learn to be graceful and feminine. You walk like a lumberjack."

The rest of that day I made it a point to flit and leap, waving my hands above my head and giving off whirring sounds. Grandma, my mother's mother, was living with us. She was a widow. She had run away from an arranged marriage and also from something called pogroms (I thought Pogroms was the name of a place) in Russia when she was sixteen, a long time ago, but her English still left something to be desired. Though she spoke Russian, German, Hebrew and Yiddish, and knew a little Polish and Rumanian, her English had obviously been grudgingly acquired out of necessity rather than inclination. She had gone to night school for a term to learn the English alphabet so we could identify her preserves, thereafter labeled phonetically in Grandma's voice: "Blegber," "Agelber" and "Crebebl."

"St. Vita's dance she's got?" Grandma said to my mother after watching me for a while.

"Ignore her," my mother said.

"Your underwear itches?" she said to me.

"Whirr, whirr," I said.

"Meshugenah," she said, shrugging and returning to her labors. It was the cook's night out and Grandma's night in. She was making kreplach. If it hadn't been for Grandma, we'd have had no ethnic tone at all. For a while, I hovered about, flapping my wings and watching her. These were not your ordinary kreplach. In fact, I've never had any like them since. I've had the meat kind, boiled in soup. I've had ravioli. I've had empanadas and Chinese wontons. But these were dainty, thin-skinned pockets filled with cottage cheese, or pot cheese, or maybe both, sautéed like blintzes in sweet butter until they were slightly crisp, golden, and delicious. I wish I could find them again.

I drifted upstairs to see what David was doing, though I had a pretty good idea what it would be. I was right. He was making one of his transatlantic liners, an elaborate construction using a number of cardboard boxes of different sizes, paper cut into various shapes and colored with crayons, and a lot of paste. David was chiefly concerned with the interiors of his ships. Our father, a dress manufacturer, went to Paris once every year and sometimes twice, and occasionally we would go with our mother to see him off. He always went first-class on a deluxe ship like the *Ile de France* and had a party in his stateroom with champagne and caviar, and while the grown-ups were dealing with these, David and I would trot around exploring the ship. We never really got to see the outside of it, as it was huddled against a pier and we made our entrance through a kind of canopied and carpeted gangplank, so that we could hardly tell where shore ended and ship began. But the inside, we thought, was gorgeous, and we never really believed that all of that endless luxury would actually float. It was like a fairy tale.

So what David was intent on fabricating, in painstaking detail, was the ship's innards, and only the first-class parts. We'd never seen the parts of the ship that made it work. He'd make three or four levels, but the top one was open until the very end, cross-sectioned and fitted with cubicles representing the staterooms, the dining salons, the bar, nightclub, gym, swimming pool and movie theater. He even had little bathrooms with carefully cut out toilets. I had to admire the detail. It was an achievement that took him hours, and sometimes the project spanned a whole weekend. When it was finished, he'd put a top on it with smokestacks, fill the bathtub with water, and sink the ship.

Much later I realized that what he was doing was killing our father, though I don't recall that he ever put any people in the ship. I didn't know about Oedipus then, though I was beginning to learn about other complexes. At the time I thought that David was simply doing one of those dopey destructive things boys did. Sometimes he didn't even wait to watch the ship go down. He'd leave it floating in the tub and some time later he'd come back and fish out the soggy, disintegrated mess and throw it away.

This particular day, he was working on the swimming pool when I fluttered up to watch. He had a mirror from one of our mother's handbags and was carefully fitting it into a square of cardboard.

"How was the dancing lesson?"

"I'd rather not talk about it."

"What'd they make you do?"

I flopped onto the floor and scrutinized his handiwork. He had outdone himself with the movie theater. There was even a screen with a cowboy riding a horse on it, a picture cut out of *The Saturday Evening Post.* Black and white. That was before Technicolor.

"You walked in your sleep again last night," I said. "You peed on the bathroom chair instead of in the toilet."

He looked up, interested, a pale, thin boy with a lot of curly brown hair and greenish eyes, not quite a year and a half older than me. Though we fought a lot, we were close. He didn't have any friends because he was shy and also because he didn't like to do any of the things the kids on the block did, punchball and stickball and territory. The other boys called him a sissy and shunned him. He was taking piano lessons and he was already up to "The Turkish March."

"What I'd like to know," I said, "is why you have to come wake me up and tell me you have to go to the bathroom. I can understand it when you come to tell me the house is on fire or there's a robber looking in the window. But why when you have to go to the bathroom? You know where it is."

"I really peed on the chair?"

"Why do you?"

"Pee on the chair?"

"Wake me up."

"How should I know? I'm asleep, aren't I?"

One of the things I was learning about who I was was that I was sometimes expected to be an older sister to my older brother. With none of the privileges. Because, as my mother explained from time to time, "David is so sensitive. He's not like other boys. He has a lot of fears and an inferiority complex."

"What's an inferiority complex?"

"He doesn't know his own worth."

This was a new idea, and one that surprised me, for David was always lording it over me and telling me how stupid I was.

"We have to help him gain self-confidence."

"What's that?"

"Knowing his own worth."

I thought about this for a while.

"How much *is* David worth?" I said.

It was one of my jobs when he sleepwalked into my room to unburden himself of whatever was on his mind, to fix it somehow and then see him back to his bed. If the house was on fire, I'd say, "I'll go look." Then I'd go look and tell him, "It's okay, the house isn't on fire." Or, "There's nobody at the window. If there was, he's gone away." The night before I'd led him to the toilet and gone out into the hall to wait for him. Then, when I went back in, he was standing at the chair fixing his pajama pants. The chair was at the other end of the bathroom, a white chair with a cane bottom, and there was a puddle underneath it. He must have done it on purpose, even in his sleep. But I didn't say anything; I couldn't see much point in making unnecessary conversation with a sleepwalker. I took his arm and led him back to his bed and waited for him to get into it and said, "Go to sleep," which he was anyhow the whole time, and "Good night." In the morning I got blamed.

"You'd think *I* did it," I protested.

"You shouldn't have let him," my mother said and then added, irrelevantly, "Thank God you'll be starting school soon."

Chapter 2

First grade. I was allowed to skip kindergarten. I already knew how to play.

And I could read. I had learned the alphabet off a little enamel table with the letters, painted in different hues, spanning its surface like a rainbow. I was supposed to play tea party on the little table but I never did. I played cobbler on it, hammering nails into my shoes. I played operations on it, cutting open my dolls. I played torture on it, tying my unoperated-on dolls onto the top of the table and burning their toes, threatening worse if they didn't confess. These were educational pastimes because meanwhile, without being aware of it, I was learning the alphabet.

Then one night when I was four and my mother was reading to me I had an overwhelming curiosity about whether the squiggles on the pages really said what she said they said. I grabbed the book out of her hands and looked at the squiggles and they weren't squiggles at all. They really did say "Arabella had a blue ball and Araminta had a red ball," as clear as looking at a tree and seeing a tree.

"I'll read to *you,"* I said, and did.

My mother thought I had memorized the book so she ran downstairs and got another.

"It was the best of times, it was the worst of times," I read. "I think this is going to be more interesting than Arabella and Araminta."

I had also picked up some business arithmetic. My father talked about money a lot. He was always talking about how much money he was losing that season or asking my mother how much she had paid per pound for that lousy piece of meat, so it was almost impossible not to learn which numbers were more than others, and how much more.

Also a sprinkling of foreign tongues.

"Geb cocken offen yom."

Grandma made an effort to look horrified.

"Where did you hear such a thing?"

"Is it dirty?"

"In this house you didn't hear it."

Technically I had, though it had carried from next door. One of our breakfast room windows faced across our alley to the Seltzers' kitchen, a lively place. Mama and Papa Seltzer were a squat, bear-shaped, lowering pair with powerful lungs passed on to their nine children. There had been ten children, but one of them had fallen out of an upstairs window. In that house, everyone made his own breakfast. One by one they would wander into the kitchen and putter around trying to stir up a meal. There was a lot of traffic and it gave rise to many battles. On warm days with the windows open, David and I picked up some interesting Yiddish, all curses.

"Tell me what it means," I said.

"Geh means go. *Cocken* means to move the bowels. *Yom* is the ocean."

"Go move your bowels in the ocean?" I said. "That's what it means?"

"It's a saying."

Why would Morty Seltzer tell Sylvia Seltzer to go move her bowels in the ocean because she asked for the frying pan?

All my dealings with Sylvia Seltzer, who was my age, had been unsatisfactory. We had tried to be friends. I had been inside her house several times and hated it. It smelled of fried onions and it was messy and cheerless, dark and over-populated. You couldn't take a step without bumping into someone, even in the bathroom. The chief thing I learned from Sylvia is that sometimes, for no apparent reason, it can happen that two people simply don't like each other. She didn't like my face, my manner or the things I said, and I didn't like her inflections, or anything about her voice. Her vowels were all in her nose and her consonants came out of her teeth, mixed with saliva. Neither of us knew enough to call the whole thing off, so we grew more and more irritated with each other, until one day Sylvia glared at me and said, "You wanna fight?"

"Sure," I said, glaring back.

"Not now, dummy. A *real* fight, with rules. Just to prove."

"Okay."

"I'll let you know when."

The call came on the morning of a day when my mother had left orders for Arthur to drive David and me to the Black Willow Golf Club where, when she finished her eighteen holes, we were to have lunch with her and her friends and their children.

Sylvia and I squared off in the Seltzers' backyard surrounded by a cheering squad comprised of four of Sylvia's older brothers (who had coached her) and about a dozen of their friends, to whom Sylvia had sold tickets for two cents apiece. Naturally, they were all rooting for Sylvia. Her brother Morty was the referee. All I knew about fighting was to ball my fists and swing them. She beat me up.

When I got back to the house to get dressed up for my luncheon engagement, I had a black eye, a bloody nose, a cut lip and a missing tooth. The tooth had been on its way out anyway. Grandma, over the initial shock, plunged me into a hot bath, shaking her head over my ineptitude.

"This is how you fight, dumbbell," she said, taking a stance in the middle of the bathroom floor. "With the head down. The left arm up like this. Jumping around on the toes. Sideways. Backwards. Forwards. In and out. And what's furthermore, stay away from that Sylvia Seltzer. She's not for you."

She patched me up as best she could, dressed me in a crisp dotted-swiss frock brought home by my father from Paris, hustled David and me into the back of the Buick and told Arthur to hurry because we were late.

"What on earth happened to you?" my mother said.

"I had a fight with Sylvia Seltzer."

"Girls don't fight. You look atrocious."

According to my mother, there was almost nothing girls were supposed to do except sit around with dolls on their laps, humming tunes. I looked at the other kids, already eating their chicken salad. One was a stunning youth about eight years old with curly black hair, olive skin and flashing dark eyes. I sat down next to him.

"I'm Allegra Maud Goldman," I told him.

He looked at me with total disinterest.

"You've got a black eye," he said, so I showed him the

space where my tooth had come out. Grudgingly, he told me that his name was Dickie Soloway.

"You want to be my boyfriend?"

"No."

"How come?"

"I hate girls," he said.

"Then how about climbing some trees after lunch?" I said.

"Girls don't climb trees," my mother, who was eavesdropping, said.

The whole day was like that. I couldn't wait for it to be over so I could start a better one.

The next morning I went outside before anyone was up. It had rained during the night and the sidewalks were still damp, but the sun was coming up and the air had a strange, beautiful light and smelled wonderful. It was spring and I felt acutely happy. The Norway maples that lined our street were freshly green, their seedpods spiralling down. I caught one in midair, fastened it to my nose and broke into a run. I ran all the way up the street to Avenue J and halfway back again before I was out of breath and had to stop. A fat boy named Willie came out of his house and said hello. He was an older boy, about twelve.

"You're wearing your pajamas," he said. I was. And my bunny slippers.

"You've got a black eye."

"I had a fight with Sylvia Seltzer. She won."

"I bet you think you're highly intelligent," he said.

"Yes," I said, though I didn't know if I was or I wasn't.

"What does inhale mean?"

"Inhale?"

He nodded.

"Are you sure you're pronouncing it right?"

"Yes. Inhale."

Stumped on the very first question!

"A lot of people have died," I said. "Some of them are in heaven and some of them are inhale."

I broke for home, leaving Willie doubled over. My first pun.

"What does inhale mean?" I asked my mother at breakfast.

"To breathe in. Exhale is to breathe out. Inhale, exhale."

It was embarrassing not to have known something as ordinary as that. I vowed that I would learn every word there was and by the time I started school I had learned quite a few.

So I skipped kindergarten. I didn't know why I couldn't skip school entirely. I never did find out. I stayed in P.S. 193 until I was twelve and a half years old, a long time, and all I got out of it was a diploma and a Palmer Method button. If anyone had told me then that high school was going to be worse, I would have run away to sea.

But I was nervous that first day. There were about twenty-five kids in the class, and it was too many people in one room. Mrs. Mendelssohn assigned us to desks in alphabetical order. I was in the third row.

"The first thing we are going to learn today is classroom etiquette," Mrs. Mendelssohn said. "Who knows what etiquette means?"

No one said anything so I said, "Etiquette is knowing which fork to use and who goes through the door first."

Mrs. Mendelssohn looked at the cards on her desk so she could figure out who I was and then she said, "Thank you, Allegra. Etiquette is also raising your hand for permission to speak. Let's try it again. Who knows what etiquette means?"

I felt I had done my share so I looked out of the window at Bedford Avenue and the houses across the street and wondered how my mother was enjoying her first day with absolutely no children in the house. Meanwhile, nobody was raising his hand.

"Allegra?"

I looked at Mrs. Mendelssohn.

"Raise your hand, Allegra," she said patiently.

I raised my hand.

"Yes, Allegra?"

"Yes what?" I said.

"Give the answer to the question you raised your hand to answer," she said.

"I raised my hand because you told me to."

"Don't argue. Just answer the question."

"Etiquette is raising your hand," I said.

There was more about hands, because when we had gotten that all straightened out, Mrs. Mendelssohn taught us how to fold them and place them on the edge of the desk and how to sit quietly at attention. I tried to stay awake.

You'll never guess what came next.

"Now, children, to help us get acquainted, we will each tell our name and our address and what we plan to be when we grow up."

Arnold Alexander was going to be a doctor. Nine out of ten boys were going to be doctors. The tenth boy was going to be a certified public accountant. It was a mostly Jewish neighborhood.

"Allegra Maud Goldman, 925 East 24th Street," I said when my turn came. "A Supreme Court justice."

You'd have thought I'd said something obscene.

"A Supreme Court justice did you say, Allegra?" Mrs. Mendelssohn said. She gave me an odd look, made a little note on what must have been my card and passed on to Harriet Horowitz, who was going to be a registered nurse.

The days went by pretty much in that vein, though there were two periods when Mrs. Mendelssohn got to rest. These were lunch and recess.

Recess was going outside to a bleak concrete yard to skip rope or choose up partners for seesaw. In the beginning, I chose a girl named Swifty because she was fat and that guaranteed that I would be instantly catapulted up, there to hang while Swifty tried to figure out how to get me down. Had she been less decent, she might have caught on and simply gotten up and walked away, leaving my descent in the hands of the natural laws of physics. Instead, after I'd put on a good show of struggling to get my end down and hers up, she would call for help and we would be told, wearily, to pick someone our own size next time.

There were other games, but some of them came later when we were more ready for them. In one, we formed a vicious circle and, whooping, hurled a volleyball at an unlucky classmate named It who was in the center of the circle, desperately trying to avoid being hit. This was a useful lesson in cruelty, meant, I imagine, to prepare us for the day when we would want to join our fellow townsfolk in stoning the village idiot to death.

Lunch. A vast subterranean chamber permeated all year with the smell of our egg salad sandwiches, which were limp by the time we withdrew them from their wrinkled brown paper bags. While our sandwiches disintegrated in our hands, we drank through straws the milk we had bought with our pennies, blowing bubbles, slurping the dregs, adding whatever we could to the echoing din. Once, just before lunch period, I looked up from my desk and there was Arthur saying something to Mrs. Mendelssohn. I had been absent for a few days with a sore throat, which Grandma had taken charge of because my parents were having a little holiday from us at The Laurel in the Pines in Lakewood, New Jersey. When I saw Arthur my first thought was that my parents had met with a fatal accident.

He came over to my desk and I saw that he was carrying two paper bags, the familiar brown kind with the grocer's pencilled scribbling on them. He thrust one at me and said, "Heah your rubbers, 'Legra. It rainin' outside." I grabbed the bag from him, mortified because everyone was watching. "And heah your lunch," he said, handing me the other bag.

"I already have my lunch," I screamed in a whisper.

"This somethin' hot your granny say for you to eat."

Inside the bag, I discovered when I got to the lunchroom, was a glass jar filled with Ukrainian borscht. Also a tablespoon. One of the kitchen spoons, in case I lost it. I dumped the whole thing into the nearest trash basket. I loved Ukrainian borscht, but if I had been caught eating it in that lunchroom, I would have been ruined socially.

In the not-too-distant future, when we were a little more mature, the tedium would be spiced with Music Appreciation and Art Appreciation. I approached Music Appreciation with a light heart. After all, I knew something about music. David played the piano. I even liked music. Miss Alenious, a Greek lady who was having a romance with Mr. Biretta, the shop teacher, informed me almost immediately that I was a listener and thereafter would have nothing to do with me except to say sharply, "Hush, Allegra, you're a listener," when, from time to time, out of sheer exuberance, I forgot and lifted my voice in song. They were such catchy tunes. "Morning is breaking / Peer Gynt is waking / morning from Peer Gynt by Grieg."

If I was a failure at dancing, music and lunch, at least I was confident that I could succeed in Art Appreciation. One thing I knew I could do better than most people was draw. I could even draw horses, which were the hardest. But alas, there wasn't any art in Art Appreciation, just appreciation. Also neatness. We were each given glossy, three-inch-square reproductions of Famous Paintings to appreciate, which we demonstrated by pasting them, without smudging, careful to leave an even quarter-inch white margin, in our Art Appreciation books, at just such a distance from the top and sides of the page, measuring with a six-inch ruler and making light pencil dots. Then we carefully, *carefully* ("Don't smear the ink!") drew borders while Mrs. Forbush gave us a short talk on why Gainsborough had painted *The Blue Boy* and why it was considered a masterpiece.

But in first grade there was little relief from Mrs. Mendelssohn and Dick and Jane and Spot, the Kallikaks of the primer. How boring it was, waiting for everyone to figure out that D-I-C-K spelled Dick. And when they had worked their way through that labyrinth what a treat was in store for them, what a tale: Dicky Dare went to school. On the way he met Jane.

"I can't stand it anymore," I told my mother after what seemed like a lifetime of this. It was one of those rare afternoons when she was at home on my return from school.

"What can't you stand?"

"We're still learning about Dick and Jane," I said. "Maybe I could go to trade school and learn something useful. I could be an airplane mechanic. I read in *My Weekly Reader* where the airplane industry is going to grow by leaps and bounds."

The next morning my mother went to see Mr. Kelleher, the principal. That afternoon I was sent for and told that I was now in second grade. At that rate, I figured, I could get my primary education wrapped up by the time I was ten. How wrong I was!

I went back once to see how Mrs. Mendelssohn was managing without me. She was polite, but there was no indication that she felt my loss keenly.

Chapter 3

"Are you trying to tell me there's no difference between one forty-five and quarter to two?" I said. It was hard to tell which of us was angrier.

"*And* fifteen minutes to two," David shouted. "If you'd pay attention to what I'm saying you'd know why."

"Tell me why."

"They're all three different ways of saying the same thing."

"Why do you need three ways to say the same thing when it's only about *time?*"

"*I* don't need it, stupid. I'm only trying to explain to you the way it is. Don't argue with *me.*"

"Okay. Start all over again, and not too fast."

"When you're using numbers," David said, his voice modulating to professorial, "you're talking about minutes. Two fifteen means fifteen minutes after, or past, two. However, when you use words like half and quarter, you're talking about fractions of the hour."

"Why don't you say two and a half? I never yet heard anyone say two and a half."

"Because you say two thirty or half-past two. That's just the way it happens to be."

"Don't scratch," I said, watching his hand.

We both had chicken pox, and for the occasion David had been put in the other bed in my room so that we could keep each other company during our travail, and also so that we could remind each other not to scratch, which would leave us scarred for life. I don't know whether it was his idea or mine that he teach me to tell time. I was good at adding, I could manage some simple subtraction, and a few days earlier, using an apple, David had taught me about fractions. But time confused me because it wasn't really *about* anything and because of the language that went with it.

"Now I'm going to set the clock," David said, "and you tell me what it says." He turned the big black hands on the old kitchen clock our mother had given him to take apart since it no longer worked, and then he held it up for me to see.

I studied it, thinking of all the possibilities.

"Seventy minutes after one," I said.

He almost threw the clock at me. "What do you mean, seventy minutes after one?" he screamed. "It's ten minutes after two!"

"I know it's ten minutes after two. But it's also seventy minutes after one. Why can't I say it that way?"

"Because you can't. Once you're finished with one hour you have to talk about the next hour. You're driving me crazy."

"Try another," I said and he did.

"One third after eleven," I said.

"TWENTY MINUTES AFTER ELEVEN!"

"That's a third," I said.

"There. Are. NO. Thirds. In. Time," he said. "There are only halves and quarters. Those are the *only* fractions in time. And only ONE quarter and ONE half. And do not argue with me because I did not make it up, that is the way it is."

"I can't remember those rules," I sighed, sick of the subject. "I wonder what makes chicken pox itch."

"I wonder why they call it chicken pox. Do you think chickens get it?"

"Maybe it's something you get from chickens."

"We haven't got any chickens."

"Maybe from eating chicken. We eat chicken a lot."

"I doubt it. Why would anyone eat it then?"

"You can only get it once. Lamb-chop pox," I said. "Hamburger pox. Mashed-potato pox."

David began to giggle. "Hot-roast-beef-sandwich-with-french-fried-potatoes pox," he said. "Gefillte-fish-with-a-carrot-on-top-and-red-horseradish pox."

By this time we were both laughing so hard that Grandma appeared in the doorway, frowning. "All that screaming again," she said. "Why always fighting?"

"We're not fighting, Grandma, we're laughing."

"So tell me the joke please. I could use a little laughing myself."

"Lox pox," David gasped and we both laughed so hard we nearly fell out of bed.

"Lox pox?" Grandma said. "That's a joke?"

But we had a lot of time to pass and sometimes we did fight.

"I wonder why they only made two sets of people," I said one day. "You'd think they could have thought up more of a variety than just men and women."

"That's all they needed," David said.

"If they only made what they needed," I said, "how come they made mosquitoes?"

"For birds to eat."

"Why couldn't they think up something better for birds to eat? Something that doesn't bother people?"

"I don't know why they made *girls,*" David said, crankily. His temperature was still over 101°, though mine had dropped to almost normal. "They're dopey and they talk too much."

"You're just jealous."

"Why should I be jealous? Tell me one good thing about being a girl. Girls don't even have penises."

"What's so great about penises? Girls have vaginas."

"Penises are *some*thing, at least."

"Penises are silly, dangling out like that. At least vaginas are safely tucked away inside where they belong. And penises weren't even made right to begin with. As soon as you're born they have to cut off a piece of it."

"They don't *have* to. It's because of the Jewish religion. It's more sanitary that way."

"See? Penises aren't even sanitary. There's no part of a girl that has to be cut off to make *them* sanitary."

"That's because it's already been cut off. All they've got left is a hole."

"It is not."

"It is too."

"A cave isn't just a hole," I shouted. "It's what's around it that makes it a cave. And what about a bagel? It may have a hole in the middle but if you took away the bagel it would just be air, not a bagel."

"Yeah, but what's a vagina for, tell me that. You don't even pee out of it."

I racked my brains but I couldn't remember if anyone had

ever mentioned what vaginas were for. When I had asked my mother why girls didn't have penises, she said because they have vaginas, and as far as I could recall that had been all there was to that conversation.

"You can't even pee standing up," David said, and while I was hating him I was also making a mental note to question my mother further.

She came into the bathroom that night while I was brushing my teeth and leaned over to kiss me on the top of my head.

"Good night, sweetie," she said.

"You going out?"

"Yes. Daddy's working late and I'm going to a bridge game at Ethel's."

"Okay. Wait a minute." I rinsed my mouth and spat. "What are vaginas for?" I said.

"What are they for? Oh. Well, when women have babies, that's where they come out. Good night, dear."

And she was gone. I stood in the middle of the bathroom floor. I felt around for the proper opening. A whole baby come out of there? There must be some mistake. But why would my mother have made it up? Maybe when babies were first born they came out like toothpaste and then, in the open air, swelled into their natural shape.

When I got back into bed, I thought and thought and thought. Most of the thoughts were black, but then one came to me that was cheering.

"David," I said. "Are you awake? Penises are for making peepee and vaginas are for making people."

"Very funny," he said.

"You want me to tell you a Beginning while you're falling asleep? I thought of a new one."

"Okay, but keep it short."

"Ever since time began," I said, "people had nothing to do but go out in the forest to hunt and fight. They would come home to their caves all tired out and lie down on the floor where they would eat and then fall asleep. But there was a young maiden named Mona who didn't care much for hunting and fighting or even for standing over the fire cooking dinosaur steaks. What she liked best to do was to listen to things. She liked to go into the forest and listen to the wind and the birds and the rain. One day while she was doing this, she came upon a rock with an odd shape. She climbed onto the rock and stood on it for a while and then, by accident, she discovered that if she bent her knees and put her rear end on a flat part of the rock and her back against another part that rose straight up, and her feet dangling straight down from the knees, it was a very comfortable way to be and she could listen even better. After she had been doing this for a while, her sister Nona happened along and, seeing Mona, began to laugh.

" 'What are you doing, Mona?' Nona inquired. 'How peculiar you look.'

"Mona thought for a while, trying to find a word for what it was she was doing. Clearly, she was neither standing up nor lying down.

" 'I'm sitting,' she said. 'I just invented it.'

" 'Sitting?' Nona said.

" 'Yes. That is the word for what I am doing. You have to bend your body in this way. It's comfortable. Would you like to try it?'

"She got up and showed Nona how to do it. She too liked it.

" 'What a lovely invention,' she said. 'It's too bad we can't do it in our cave.'

" 'I was just thinking the same thing,' Mona said. 'It would certainly be a better way to eat. Also, it gives us a new part of our body that we never had before.' She pointed out the space between Nona's hips and her knees. 'I think we will call that a lap.'

" 'Why a lap?' Nona inquired.

" 'Why not?' said Mona. 'It's a sound that isn't being used for anything else.' "

"How about what a cat does with milk in a saucer?" David said.

"This is before saucers," I said. "It's even before that kind of milk. Shall I go on?"

David didn't answer so I went on.

" 'Lap. Lap,' Nona said, memorizing it.

" 'I think a lap will come in very handy when we have our babies, don't you?' Mona said. 'I mean, we could be sitting on our rock and the baby could be sitting on our lap while we sing to it.'

" 'If only more rocks came in this particular shape,' Nona said, sighing. 'And if only they were't too heavy to roll into our cave.'

"But Mona was still thinking. If you have a searching mind, one invention will lead to another.

" 'Why could we not,' she said thoughtfully, 'fashion something in this shape out of a lighter material? The logs of a tree, for example.'

"So in the next days Mona and Nona were busy with their axes and hammers and nails, and they figured out what was the best way to do it. And when they had done it they thought up a name for it. Because it was a happy invention, they wanted it to have a cheerful name.

" 'What about calling it a cheer?' Nona said. And so they did, only in the years to come it got changed, probably by way of Scotland, into chair.

"When they had made one of these that suited them, they decided to make one for each member of the family. This they did in secret, as it occurred to them that the cheers would make a nice surprise for their father, whose birthday was coming up on Tuesday. They worked very hard and by Monday night they had completed four serviceable cheers. Tuesday morning it looked like rain for a while, so nobody left the cave. But at around two o'clock in the afternoon the sun came out, so their father and mother went out into the forest to hunt and fight, and while they were gone Mona and Nona stole to their secret place and carried the cheers into the cave where, after pushing aside the skins, they set them in the middle of the floor in a sort of square, all facing in. They they went to hide in a corner of the cave until their parents came back, which was fairly soon, as it did start to rain after all. Their father was grouchy because he had only had time to spear one wild boar, and a baby at that.

" 'What is all that junk,' he said. 'Really, Winona, I would think you could keep this cave a little less cluttered up.'

" 'I don't know a thing about it,' their mother exclaimed.

" 'Surprise, surprise,' the girls shouted gleefully, and, 'Happy birthday, happy birthday.'

" 'Thank you, girls,' their father said looking surprised, as he had forgotten all about it being his birthday. 'But what is all this junk?'

" 'They are not junk,' Mona said.

" 'They are cheers,' Nona said.

"And the two girls sat down, each in one of the cheers, and after their parents had circled them for a while, squinting and openmouthed in astonishment, they were persuaded to do likewise.

"'It's called sitting,' Mona explained. 'Isn't it cheerful?'

'Their parents clapped their hands joyfully.

"'And won't it be nicer to eat our dinner sitting in these cheers instead of lying down on the dirty floor?' Nona asked.

"'The floor is not dirty,' their mother said, while a thoughtful look passed across their father's face.

"'Hold everything,' he said. 'I have another idea.'"

"Doesn't this Beginning ever end?" David muttered.

"Soon," I said.

"Their father leaped out of his cheer and began to pace up and down the cave. He was not used to thinking sitting down.

"'Eureka,' he said. 'Why not?'

"He rushed out of the cave, and in a little while he was back with a flat rectangle of wood and four logs of identical length. The logs, upright, were the height of the sitters' waists and he stood them on the floor and placed the flat piece of wood over them.

"'What's that?' Winona asked.

"'I don't know its name yet,' he said, 'but it will be a handy place to put the food.' Everyone leaned over and put their elbows on it while they thought up its name.

"And that was the beginning of sitting, as well as of furniture."

"And of laps," David said.

Chapter 4

"He is not a pleasant person," I said. "I don't know what we need him for."

"You'll just have to learn to get along with him," my mother replied. We were speaking of her husband, the man she had chosen to father her children. It was Saturday morning. The scene at dinner the previous night had been, though typical, a particularly harrowing one, a virtual rout, during which my mother had been reduced to tears, Grandma to saying "Shah, shah," I to impotent anger. David had turned white and slipped out. Later, he sleepwalked twice during the night.

My father was an angry man, always blowing up about something, a hollerer. It wasn't that he had a short fuse; I think he had no fuse at all, that choler was his natural state. Everyone was afraid of him.

"There is no way to get along with him," I said. "He's only

happy when he's angry. For example, what was *that* all about last night?"

He had come home from his long day at The Place with his usual coming-home face, that of an army general who has spent the whole day trying to whip together a victorious force out of incompetents, cripples, goldbricks, insubordinates and, above all, traitors. He was coming home, his face said, to more of the same.

I suppose I ought to describe my father, but it isn't easy. Sometimes over the years he seemed one thing and sometimes another. He was a good-looking man, strong and ruddy. When I was little he seemed tall to me, but by the time I was thirteen he had become medium. He was broad-shouldered and bull-necked, an aggressively built man, with blue eyes and a broken nose, though he had never in his life been in an actual fight. His younger brother Irwin had accidentally broken my father's nose with a baseball bat (the only admission, and that inadvertent, that anyone of his generation had ever had time to play). Later, of course, I learned that there is no such thing as an accident. The victim can *meet* with an accident (if I am walking along Park Avenue and someone is being defenestrated on the eighteenth floor of the Waldorf Astoria and falls on me, I defy anyone to find anything in my psyche to make me a party to my own demise), but the perpetrator is something else again. And considering my father's personality, it is hard to believe that something in Irwin's unconscious hadn't made him careless of the fact that my father's nose was within range of that bat. I once nearly put David's eye out with a niblick, and though I was sick to my stomach the moment the club made that hideous soft contact, and beside myself with remorse and even panic, I am willing to consider that there were devils at work within me, as I am not without complexity.

When he came home on this particular night, David and I were playing Ride. We'd put a blanket at the top of the stairs and one of us would sit in the middle of it. Then the other would pull the front end of the blanket, running down the stairs. The one on the blanket would, therefore, make the descent bump, bump, bump, on his behind. Because the stairs were carpeted, Ride was not as painful as it would otherwise have been, but there was still no way to play it without laughing hysterically.

"Cut that out!" our father said first thing, ignoring our "Hello, Daddy." "You'll tear the blanket." No concern for us. We might have cracked our spines. "You think blankets grow on trees?"

"No, on sheep," David said under his breath, but we cut it out while our father went upstairs to wash, grumbling about how he slaved away all day to make a few dollars only to come home to find his own flesh and blood destroying his property.

We went meekly into the dining room for dinner. Eventually we were supposed to inherit the earth, but meanwhile there were some bridges to cross.

"Why does she have to look like that?" was the next thing. It was said to our mother, concerning me. I waited for my mother to answer, interested in what she might come up with. As she chose not to say anything at all, I said, "Like what?"

"Why can't she comb her hair?" my father said to my mother. Again, my mother was silent.

"She just combed it," I answered for her, exasperated. "She can't help it. It grows crooked."

He turned his attention then to the chicken noodle soup and the afternoon mail, which he had brought with him to the table. For a while, except for the rending of envelopes and the inhaling of soup, there was silence.

"Bills, bills, bills," he said, finally. "Christ, Tess, don't you know how to do anything but spend money?"

"What kind of bills?" my mother said, at last stung to reply. "For the coal, the telephone, and the electricity? Do you expect me to run a home for five people plus two in help without spending any money?"

"If just one of you learned to turn the goddamned lights off when you go out of a room," he said, grasping at straws. "And what's this item here on this bill from Abraham & Straus?"

My mother studied it.

"That's underwear for David."

"You just bought him underwear, fachrissake. How much underwear does one person need, a child?" His voice was increasing in volume. He was finding his range.

"I didn't just buy *him* underwear. That was for Allegra. They're growing children."

My father's bureau was full of underwear. And shirts. You never saw so many shirts, and all of them with monograms on the pockets.

"You begrudge your only son underwear?" I said.

"What? *What!* I won't have that little snotnose talk to me that way. I didn't work like a dog all my life to have some little snotnose brat who hasn't brought in her first dollar yet talk to me like that."

"My first *dollar*," I shrieked. "I'm still a child."

"By the time I was your age, I'd been working three years already." This was not news to me. I can't tell you how many times I had heard about it. My father's parents had owned a little grocery store, and as soon as my father could see, they had set him to candling eggs.

My Grandma and Grandpa Goldman. I believe my father

spent a good part of his life repaying them for their kindness, frequently by way of David and me. Not Grandpa, who actually was kind, but who was so timid and ineffectual that he didn't count for my father; but Grandma, who was the power, the ruling force. It was easy to understand why my father could not allow even a whiff of matriarchy in his own household.

"All you kids know is to play," my father hammered on. "*I* never had time to play. When I was your age . . ."

I tried to picture my father as a child but it was impossible. I could only picture him exactly as he then was, fully developed, but smaller. A midget. I even tried to get him out of business suits and into some other kind of clothing, but at this, too, I failed. Since almost all of his activities at our age, or at least those we were told about, were devoted to the pursuit of nickels and pennies, as the idea was at all times to be "productive" (his word), I had a number of images in my head of this truncated version of the man now sitting at the head of our table, ranging from two to four feet high, unsmiling and intense, engaged in egg candling, or selling rides to the neighborhood kids on one of his Uncle Moe's nanny goats (Uncle Moe made cheese), or delivering delicatessen for his Uncle Julius. Although much of this sounds pastoral, it all took place on the streets of New York City, specifically the Lower East Side's streets, not exactly farmland, though often referred to by my father as a jungle.

"My idea of *playing*," he said, "of having *fun*, when I was just taking it *easy*, was to shovel the horse manure in the streets into cigar boxes and sell it for fertilizer."

It was a difficult picture to add to my collection, but there it was, this midget in a gray flannel suit with a white pinstripe, collecting horse manure on Rivington Street.

"Where could you sell fertilizer in New York City?" David asked with disbelief.

"There were still farms around in those days. You didn't have to go too far. If you're enterprising you can find a use for anything. But what would you kids know! All you know is to tear up blankets."

"You want us to collect horse manure?" I said. "You want us to hang around in the gutter hoping some horse will come along and move its bowels so we can put it in a box? I never heard of anything so disgusting."

My father turned purple. "There she goes again," he shouted. "With that big mouth. Can't you teach her a little respect? If I'd ever talked to my parents like that they'd have killed me."

"Children should be seen and not heard," my mother contributed grimly, ganging up on me. That was the worst part, having her join the enemy. I knew it was her idea of diplomacy, and that it probably stemmed from cowardice, but to me it was simple betrayal, selling out her own child for the sake of peace.

"I don't understand any of you," I shouted. It made me mad to know that pretty soon I would be crying. "We live in a corner house with three bathrooms and a Buick and a chauffeur and a cook and a mother who plays cards or mah-jongg practically every single minute, and you expect your seven-year-old child to go out looking for work?"

"I expect you to keep your mouth shut," my father bellowed. "Except to put food in it bought with the sweat of my brow."

"Shah, shah," Grandma the peacemaker said. "It's enough already."

"And she's right," my father said, turning on my mother,

"You're all a bunch of useless parasites."

"That's not what I said," I screamed, trembling with every rotten kind of strong emotion. It was time to throw down my napkin and storm out. David had already slipped away. I think these scenes were hardest on him because he was a boy. He was supposed to grow up to follow in our father's footsteps, and of course that was out of the question. My problem was that I was supposed to grow up to be like my mother, and that was out of the question, too, since it might mean having to be married to someone like my father. But it was simpler for me because I had already decided not to. I was going to find something else to be, though I hadn't yet figured out what.

So there I was, discussing the problem with my mother the following day, and she was being unsatisfactory. For one thing, we were not simply sitting down having a nice little heart-to-heart, vis-à-vis. It was rarely possible to arrange that with my mother. She was hardly ever home. When she was, it was because there was something that had to be done. If I wanted to talk to her, I had to trot around at her heels, thankful for whatever fraction of her attention was available to me. Most often our conversations took place in the brief intervals between lengthy telephone conversations with her chums, of whom there were many and from whom, at the moment, she was unhappily separated owing to the pressures of "family life." It was a terrible frustration for me, trying to get some important point across against such odds. There were times when I would have liked to strap her to a chair. This was one of them.

It was spring. She was taking winter garments out of closets and preparing to make them unappetizing to moths. There had already been phone calls from Jenny and Ethel. They were arranging a game. They were forever arranging games, except for the Monday game and the Friday game, which were fixed and only had to be rearranged when one of the regulars couldn't make it because of some bothersome intrusion like a disease or a funeral.

"He's a self-made man," my mother said. "That's how they are."

A self-made man. That, too, I had been hearing for as long as I could remember. In the beginning it had conjured up a literal image of a hand and arm rising slowly from a doughy mass, the hand then reaching down into the mass, from which it proceeded, painstakingly, blindly, to sculpt itself, my father.

"What *is* a self-made man?" I asked, and for a moment my mother looked startled. When you label something, you don't really have to think about it.

"A self-made man is one who, well, I guess you could say starts with nothing and becomes a success."

"How can you start with nothing?" I argued. "He had a mother and father, and food, clothing and shelter, didn't he?"

"Yes, but he didn't have the advantages many people have. Help from his parents. Money. Comfort. Schooling."

My father could have had more schooling if he had wanted it. He went to school to get what he thought he would need in the workaday world: business arithmetic and a handwriting. He quit in his first year of high school when they got to *Treasure Island*. There was no way he could see of putting *Treasure Island* to practical use.

"If he had to make himself," I said, "why couldn't he have made himself nicer?"

"Nobody's perfect," my mother said. "You'll have to learn to get along with him."

"You can't learn to get along with him," I said, "any more than you can learn to get along with a volcano."

39

I had come across a picture book about Pompeii a few days earlier. It had made a strong impression on me. An artist had recreated the last days. There was one particularly vivid picture in full and living color: a small family, man, woman, child and dog, running like hell, looking back over their shoulders in terror at the molten lava thundering after them, already nipping at their heels, knowing that in a moment it would engulf them. That had really happened. There were photographs of the ruins and of bodies reconstructed from the molds formed by real bodies once encased in the lava that had since hardened.

"Your father isn't a volcano," my mother said.

"There isn't a thing in the world you can do to stop it," I said. "It's a force of nature."

"Your father isn't a force of nature," my mother said. "He doesn't understand children because he never had a childhood himself."

"I know of plenty of fathers who are nice to their own children. Who even *love* them." Actually, at that time I could think of only one, Florence Hirsh's father, a sweet, gentle man who, since he was a lawyer, probably hadn't had such a deprived boyhood. Florence Hirsh lived halfway up the block, and I disliked going to her house because, if her father happened to be home, whenever he just *looked* at Florence his face melted with love. For some reason this made me feel like crying and pretty soon I would be picking a fight with Florence.

"Your father does love you," my mother insisted. "He just doesn't know how to show it. And when he comes home at night he's tired. He works too hard."

"Who asked him?" I said. "Did you? Did I? He works too

hard because he can't help it any more than a live volcano can keep from blowing up."

"I wish I knew what you were talking about," my mother said. "Are you trying to be poetic?"

"Well, don't say I didn't warn you," I said. "He's already ruined David's life, and I don't know how much longer I'm going to be able to keep *my* head above water."

This got to her. She looked up from one of my father's suits that she'd been inspecting, trying to decide if it needed to go to the cleaners before being bagged and balled in the cedar closet.

"What are you talking about?"

"David is a nervous wreck," I said. "Scared of his own shadow."

"He was born that way," my mother said. She threw the suit down on the bed and lit a cigarette. "He was a colicky baby. He cried all the time. When he was just an infant in his carriage if a man with a beard passed by, he would scream with terror. He couldn't even have known what a beard *was*. What has that got to do with your father, to say nothing of volcanos?"

The telephone rang again, and I sat half listening while my mother and Mildred discussed who they were going to invite to a joint luncheon they were giving next Wednesday at the Black Willow Country Club. But I was still thinking about Pompeii. It was beginning to dawn on me that if my analogy was valid, and I was sure it was, the only sensible thing to do was flee before it was too late.

I went to my room and got a book; I took a blanket out of the linen closet; I went to the basement for a flashlight; I filched a box of Oreos from the pantry. They were not my favorite cookie, but they were all I could find. I put all these items in a shopping bag, trying not to think yet about where I was going or what I was going to do when I got there. As I've mentioned, I hated long walks, and for a moment it crossed my mind that I could get Arthur to drive me. Then I thought about going on my roller skates, but I hadn't been able to find my skate key all week.

I went to find David, which was no problem, as he was practicing the piano. He had been taking this measure over and over again, a difficult one full of grace notes in the right hand and complicated chords in the bass. You would think something like that would be annoying to others, but it never was to me. I liked it; it was comforting. The sound of David's practicing, no matter what it was, had become background, like the sound of the sea, or the humming of insects and the twittering of birds in a meadow. It had gotten so that when he wasn't practicing, I missed it.

He didn't look up when I went into the living room. The last of that day's sunlight slanted through the windows behind him, a strange weak light with motes dancing in it. It made David look ethereal, almost like a ghost. I watched him for a minute, listening, feeling sorry about leaving him because he looked so frail, and feeling responsible for him. What I was going to do seemed selfish. Also, he was so much a part of my life that I knew I was going to miss him.

"I hate to interrupt you, David," I said, "but I wanted to say good-bye."

"Good-bye," he said, his hands and eyes still on the music. "Where are you going?"

"I'm leaving home."

"Well, so long," he mumbled. "Have a good trip."

"I think you should come, too," I said. "Before it's too late."

"Can't. My lesson's tomorrow and I have to practice."

I hadn't really thought he would come.

I got back up to my parents' bedroom just as my mother was hanging up the telephone.

"I came to tell you good-bye," I said.

"Where do you think you're going?"

"A volcano is a mountain," I said. "You can't move a mountain and you can't stop a volcano from erupting. The only thing you can do is move yourself."

She laughed and this made me angry. Downstairs, I put on my new suede jacket and then deliberately took off the front-door key, which I wore on a string around my neck, and left it on the telephone table where it would be sure to be seen. In case they had any illusions about my coming back.

Outside, the kids had interrupted their stickball game to cluster around the Velvet Ice Cream wagon, which, though painted bright orange, was pulled by a dispirited brown horse named Tony and driven by Joe, a sad-eyed, unsmiling Italian with a huge drooping moustache. The wagon's slow passage, its wake marked by Tony's occasional droppings and a narrow rivulet of melting ice, was announced by a bell that tolled rather than tinkled. Into fluted paper cups of varying sizes, depending on what you were prepared to pay (from two cents all the way up to a nickel), Joe dispensed two shades of Italian ice and ice cream in the three basic flavors, along with a flat wooden spoon shaped so.nething like the paddle of a kayak.

The kids were handing up their pennies, shouting their orders: "A two-cents chawklit." "Gimme a nickel vanella." But I walked right past them as though I had already put behind me not only my family, but my neighborhood. I walked up the street to Avenue J, turned left one block to Bedford Avenue, and then started ambling down Bedford, trying to decide what to do. It was already nearly dusk. By the time I got to the Spieglemans' house I had figured out that I didn't really have to go very far, just as long as they didn't know where I was, in the unlikely event that they would come to miss me and try to fetch me back. The Spieglemans' house was directly behind ours, separated by their backyard and ours. I walked up their alley and around behind their garage. Our garages were back to back, too, with a space between about two feet wide. I entered this space, spread my blanket there, and sat down on it. Feeling snug and secure and safely hidden, I opened the box of Oreos and the book and began to consume both.

It was a new book, and it gripped me. It was about a poor unwanted waif. He's huddled in a doorway freezing to death, but he has this big furry dog, and while the boy sleeps the dog covers him with his big furry body, shielding him from the wind and the snow, so that in the morning, when the boy wakes up, he is alive thanks to the dog, but the dog has frozen to death. I cried. By flashlight. And then I realized that I was crying not only for the dead dog and that poor unwanted child (everything came out all right for him in the end; he turned out to be the long-lost child of someone rich and noble), but for myself. Self-pity, my mother called it. No matter what I cried about my mother always called it self-pity, which to her was something loathsome, though I have never to this day understood why. There are times when we are indeed pitiful, and why shouldn't we be the first to know it?

Then I got to thinking about those Pompeians and I stopped crying. I wondered why they had chosen to live in the shadow of Vesuvius and to build their city there. Maybe in the beginning they hadn't known it was a volcano. Or maybe they were superstitious and felt they could placate the gods, that if they were destroyed by the volcano it would be because they had angered the gods. Still, Vesuvius must have rumbled before blowing up and given all kinds of warnings. Why hadn't they gotten out in time? And hadn't others come along and rebuilt a new city on top of the old ruins and gone right on living there? To this very day? And weren't there people in other parts of the world, India especially, who went on living in the paths of floods that rampaged like clockwork, predictably, every year in the monsoon season, wiping out thousands? Why didn't they simply pick up and leave? Was it because home—the land, the house, the people—was something more than a place, an integral part of themselves?

Was it simply that they had nowhere else to go?

It was a difficult question for me. I brooded over it for a long time. The Oreos had given out. I would starve before morning. What was the point of fleeing one disaster only to perish from another? Out of the frying pan into the fire, Grandma would say. I wondered what I had missed for dinner.

I knew then that I couldn't escape it. Not yet. I was doomed to that house, those parents, my brother, this street, this borough. They were my fate. They were who I was.

That's the way he is, I told myself. After all, he *is* my father and not a natural disaster. Things might have been worse. I made myself think of ten different ways it could have been worse and it was easy. There must be a way I could survive; there must be a way I could separate myself other than physically. I could read all the time. While I was reading I wasn't where I actually was, I was where it was in the book. I would read, I would be wary and I would grow up.

I went to the back door. The lights were still on in the kitchen. I had thought it was much later than that. I tapped on the door and Olga, the cook, let me in. She was a cheerful, plump Norwegian with a round, red face, and when she smiled she covered her mouth with her hand because she was missing some teeth. When she saw me, she covered her mouth with her hand.

"I keep warm your dinner," she said.

It was meat loaf, mashed potatoes and creamed spinach. It was excellent. The kitchen was warm and the sound of the radio drifted in from the living room. Herbert Hoover was making a speech and my father would be listening and approving.

While I was still at the kitchen table, finishing my dinner, my mother came in.

"Are you back to stay?" she said.

"I wish I had a dog," I said.

"What next!" my mother said.

Chapter 5

Because of my mother's weak stomach, David was seeing a psychiatrist.

Three or four times a month, my mother had a "bad night": indigestion and nausea that kept her up most of the night and laid her low most of the following day. Periodically she would become convinced that she had at least an ulcer, probably worse. But the doctors she consulted invariably assured her, after tests and X-rays, that there was nothing wrong with her. What she had, they said, was a nervous stomach.

She tried all kinds of diets and special pills. For a while she even gave Christian Science a whirl. I don't know how deeply she went into it, but the house filled up with a quantity of literature, which I never actually saw her read. I tried to and it was pretty boring, so I suspect she didn't have the concentration for it.

At about that time, the news was out that an old Jewish man with a beard had dreamed up a whole new science in Vienna, something fantastic that could cure just about everything. My mother got wind of it, possibly through *The Ladies' Home Journal,* which she did read (it taught her how to be your typical American housewife and mother, something she had failed to learn from her Russian-born parents with their old-world eccentricities), and before long she turned up a real live practicing psychiatrist.

I didn't know about it right away. It was one of those things you weren't supposed to be perfectly candid about, as people who dealt with psychiatrists were commonly thought to be crazy. But after a while this tall, boney, sand-colored man named Dr. Dendritch took to hanging around our house. The science was still so new, at least in our neighborhood, that I don't think all the ground rules had been laid yet. Probably even Freud hadn't learned that you weren't supposed to hang around your patients' homes, that it was better to keep a cool, professional distance. Or maybe Dr. Dendritch was an early splinter. My own impression was that he had fallen in love with my mother. He brought her pictures he had painted, disgusting thick globs of muddied colors, mostly browns and grays. He would look around our walls and decide where the latest picture ought to go and hang it there himself. Then he would stand back and admire it and ask me if I liked it. Usually I shrugged, trying to be polite.

"What do you think it's a painting of?" he asked me once.

"Spit and b.m.," I said.

He turned and looked at me, a long speculative look pregnant with analysis. He never asked me for an interpretation again.

After that visit, I asked my mother just who he was.

"Dr. Dendritch is a doctor I'm seeing," she said redundantly. "He's helping me with my stomach."

"How?" I asked. "That painting he brought today is enough to make anyone sick."

"The painting is a gift. It has nothing to do with the treatment."

"Tell me about the treatment."

"You're too young to understand."

The subject suddenly became interesting.

"Give me a rough idea," I said.

"We talk."

"You both sit around and talk about your *stomach?*" I asked. I tried to imagine it. What could they find to say after the first round?

"I told you you wouldn't understand," my mother said.

"Well, *explain.*"

"It's complicated," she said, sighing. "You see, the body and the mind aren't two separate entities. What we think and feel can sometimes affect our bodies and make us ill. I have a nervous stomach, which means that in certain situations, for certain reasons, my stomach acts up and makes me sick. Dr. Dendritch and I are trying to discover what those situations are and what I think and feel when I'm experiencing them. Are you following this?"

"So far," I said.

"I'm trying to make it as simple as I can. The point is, once you understand what's really happening, you can fix it. Sometimes just understanding it will make it go away."

The next time I saw my mother, which was about three days later, as our paths failed to cross before then, I had a lot of questions, but she was too busy to listen to them. Dr. Dendritch came one afternoon when my mother was out, so it seemed only natural to ask him.

"Have you discovered what situations make my mother's

stomach act up?" I asked. He looked startled and forgot to go on unwrapping that week's painting.

"I beg your pardon?" he said.

"Because if you haven't, I can tell you," I said. "It's when my father yells, which is a lot of the time. And it's also when my mother has to help my father entertain out-of-town buyers. Even though that's about the only time my father is as sweet as he can be, it makes my mother nervous to entertain out-of-town buyers."

"Did your mother discuss this with you?" Dr. Dendritch said.

"Is it supposed to be a secret?"

"Well, no."

"Anyway, those are the times. What are you going to do about it?"

Dr. Dendritch was a pipe smoker. He took his pipe out of his pocket and fussed with it. By the time he got it in his mouth and going, he seemed more relaxed.

"You're very precocious, Allegra," he said. "And you're old enough to understand that some things are private, that your mother is entitled to some privacy, just as you are. There are some things, aren't there, Allegra, that you'd rather not discuss with your mother because they're your very own private things?"

I tried to think what some of these might be, as I was perfectly willing to go on with the discussion, but Dr. Dendritch had turned his back and was fussing with the picture. It was clear that he had said all he meant to say on the subject.

"If you want my advice," I couldn't help saying, "I doubt that my mother's stomach will get better until she's married to someone different."

Dr. Dendritch seemed to shudder, and then he mumbled

something that might have been, "Thank you, Allegra," but could as easily have been some obscure Elizabethan oath. It was so difficult to have straight, intelligent conversations with adults. They were so skilled at evasion. There was nothing to do but throw up my hands in disgust and go outside to play. A new girl on the block, Lenore (pronounced LEE-naw) was giving me problems of my own. Though I had always been the leader among my peers on the block, the director of activities (years later it would be explained to me that this was only natural, owing to my being a Leo), Lenore was really bossy. If you didn't do things her way, she'd give you a cold, superior look and make her departure. It was true that she was even older than David, but still. Her favorite game was School, and of course she always insisted on being the teacher. I thought it idiotic to play at being a pupil, which in real life I had to spend so much of my time actually being. I hated playing School with Lenore. I hated playing School altogether. But Lenore held a certain fascination for me. It was a challenge trying to bend her to my will, and so far I had had absolutely no success.

It was a week before Dr. Dendritch showed up again. I was late getting home from school, having loitered on the way. As usual, my mother wasn't home. I found Dr. Dendritch wandering around one end of the living room while David was trying to practice at the piano end. I couldn't help feeling a little sorry for both of them.

"My mother's never home on Friday afternoons, Dr. Dendritch," I said, trying to be helpful. "Except when the Friday game happens to be here."

"I know that, Allegra. I saw your mother this morning in my office."

I was perplexed. I knew my mother went to see Dr. Dendritch several mornings a week for "sessions." Why, then, did he come around to the house, even when he knew she wasn't going to be there?

Dr. Dendritch went over to the piano and leaned his elbows on top of it, looking down at David, his face arranged to convey benevolence. I could tell this made David uncomfortable.

"You really like to play the piano, don't you, David," he said.

"Mmmm," David said.

"It's such a beautiful day. Wouldn't you like to take a walk with me?"

"Not right now, thank you," David said.

"Couldn't your practicing wait until later, after the sun's gone down?"

"It could," David said. "But I *feel* like practicing now."

"That's a nice piece. What's it called?"

"Mazurka," David mumbled.

Out in the street, the kids were choosing up sides for a punchball game. I considered going out to see if I could get in on it, but I couldn't tear myself away from this conversation. I was curious to learn what Dr. Dendritch was getting at.

"A Chopin mazurka?" Dr. Dendritch asked.

"Yes."

"Do you know what mazurka means, David?"

David stopped playing and looked up at Dr. Dendritch. He was all patience.

"It's a Polish dance," he explained. "Sort of a waltz, only wilder. Because of the unexpected accents." And then he waited politely to see what Dr. Dendritch would come up with next.

"Looks like a nice bunch of kids out there." He gestured

towards the window with his pipe. "Are any of them your friends?"

"I know them," David said, frowning.

"Do you play punchball?"

"Sometimes at school. When I have to."

"Don't you like to play ball?"

"Mostly, I haven't got time," David said. "Between my homework and my practicing."

I confronted my mother in her room that night before dinner. She was changing out of her mah-jongg clothes into something more comfortable.

"Why does that Dr. Dendritch hang around here so much? You see him in his office all the time, so why is he always hanging around here?"

"He's been coming here at my request," my mother said. "He's observing David in his home environment."

"What's he doing that for?"

"He thinks he can help David work out some of his problems."

"Does David know about this?"

"Not yet. And I'll be the one to tell him, if you don't mind."

"Don't you think David ought to have something to say about it? It makes him nervous, having Dr. Dendritch observe him."

"How do you know that?"

"I just got finished observing Dr. Dendritch observing David. He asked him a lot of dumb questions and kept interfering with his practicing."

"You just mind your own business," my mother said. "Dr. Dendritch knows what he's doing."

"Time will tell," I said. "Anyhow, why don't you get Dr. Dendritch to stay for dinner some time so he can see some of the real home environment that goes on around here."

"It so happens he's coming to dinner tomorrow night."

It so happened, however, that Miss Nelly Hugo also came to dinner. Miss Hugo was one of my father's favorite customers because she thought the world of my father and bought a lot of his garments. She was an aristocratic lady who, with her sister, owned a large emporium on the West Coast. Some of my father's customers, when they came to New York City to do their buying, always wanted to be taken out to dinner and the theater. Others liked a bit of home life, even ours. But Miss Hugo loved to go dancing with my father, even though she was about a hundred and twelve years old, so he always took her to some place like the Copacabana. This trip, however, she was suffering from a touch of rheumatism, so dancing was out.

Dr. Dendritch was killing two birds with one stone. He was not only observing David in his home environment, but also my mother in one of her stomach situations. Of course, owing to Miss Hugo's presence, my father was on his best behavior, and having Dr. Dendritch there seemed to make my mother more relaxed than she would otherwise have been, so I didn't think Dr. Dendritch would learn very much. I did, though. It was the first time I'd seen my father with Dr. Dendritch, and my father obviously couldn't stand him. I don't think he said two words to him all through dinner. I found my father almost loveable that night. He trotted out all his charm, which was considerable when his mind was on it, and radiated it all over Miss Hugo, who responded with adoration. I knew that if Miss Hugo had been merely a college English professor or a research biologist, he wouldn't have had much respect for her. "If she's so smart," he would have said with unanswerable logic, "why isn't she rich?" He didn't have a set of values, just this one measuring stick. He talked a lot about qualities such as ambition, industry, thrift and honesty, but if you possessed all these virtues and the world had nonetheless failed to shower you with riches because, say, you were a journeyman printer or a high school music teacher, then they didn't count. If, on the other hand, you were fantastically wealthy though a bit crooked, he would be forced to admire you.

But I was just beginning to get some inkling that money might not be everything and that my father's views might be narrow. Yet I had never been poor and he had. And he had never had time to read books and I had. I could see that if you had grown up like Oliver Twist and you were sitting down to a dinner of first-cut brisket of beef and potato pancakes and a good red wine imported from France, and the dinner had been cooked by a Norwegian lady in the kitchen, and brought home from the market by a uniformed man named Arthur in your Buick limousine that you traded in for a new one every two years, then you might feel a little smug and sure of your opinions.

So I observed my father being expansive with Miss Hugo as well as with the rest of us (except Dr. Dendritch) because we were also present. He told stories about himself when he felt good, and he was telling Miss Hugo how he had happened to marry my mother. It was a long story because it started about six years before he even met my mother when, at eighteen, he got a job in a dress factory sweeping floors. Soon, having determined that he liked the dress business, he began going to night school to learn bookkeeping so that in time he could lay down the broom and pick up a pen. Then, one day, he took a dress off the rack and told the boss, a man named Mack Julius, that the belt was all wrong, and he took a belt off another dress and said, "This is the right belt for this dress," and my father was right and Mack Julius saw that he was a born dress man and prepared to make him his son and heir, which he otherwise didn't have. He brought my father along rapidly, teaching him everything he knew, including how to eat in restaurants, as the table at which my father had grown up was set with all the cutlery in a glass jar in the middle and the food brought out in bowls, and you reached for whatever you wanted. My father had to learn to eat and otherwise comport himself properly so that he could entertain people like Miss Hugo, which in a short time he was doing. When my father had turned twenty and had learned everything, Mack Julius told him that it was time for him to settle down and get married and that he had better marry Mr. Julius's daughter.

"Not that I had anything aginst her," my father was saying. "I didn't even know her. But nobody was going to tell me who to marry, so I spit in his eye and walked out."

So far he still hadn't told how he had married my mother, but at that point Grandma began her story, which was even longer, starting practically at her birth when her father, a tavern keeper in a small town just outside Kiev, arranged her marriage to the son of the richest man in their *shtetl*, a grain merchant. The arrangement was down on paper, the terms spelled out and signed by the rabbi. It was all settled. Meanwhile, since my grandmother had to grow up, she helped out in the tavern, serving the peasants who came in from the fields; helping her stepmother in the kitchen; scrubbing the floors so you could eat off them (though they didn't); taking care of her half-sisters and brothers as they came along; and going down into the cellar (which had a dirt floor and really *was* underground) to fetch the potatoes and cabbages stored there and to listen, in passing, to the revolutionaries who met there to make plots and sing songs by the light of a candle. My grandmother's father was a learned man, so he didn't do any work except to listen to people's problems and give advice. People came from near and far.

About the time my grandmother was nearing sixteen and was going to have to marry the grain merchant's son, a young man "used to" come into the tavern, one of the peasants from the fields. "Used to" was my grandmother's past tense for anything that happened more than once. The young man was very handsome with fair hair and dark eyes, and my grandmother was very beautiful with dark hair and dark eyes, and although they never said a word to each other, they used to look at each other a lot and my grandmother knew that they loved each other. She also knew that she could never marry him, as he was a gentile and would never be anything but a peasant, except maybe a cossack, which was worse. But she also knew that she could never marry the grain merchant's son because, although she scarcely knew him either, she didn't love him. And he had blue eyes.

One of Grandma's older brothers went to America, and before leaving he whispered to her that when he had accumulated some of the gold the streets were paved with, he would send her a ticket in care of a friend of his so that it would be a secret. And he did. Just after Grandma turned sixteen she ran away, first hiding in a hay wagon, then in a rowboat, then in a fishing smack and then in some other conveyance until she finally got to the ship, where she traded in her ticket for America.

Now that both my father and grandmother had told how they had *not* married somebody, my father proceeded with the story of how he had happened to marry my mother. It came about in this way. One summer afternoon his mother was sitting on the porch of the Fleishnick Arms, a small hotel on a side street in Saratoga Springs, talking to another woman, and while they both sat sipping the mineral waters they bragged about their children. The other woman was telling Grandma Goldman about her marvelous, beautiful, intelligent daughter Tess, the most popular girl in Eastern District High School as well as secretary of the G.O. and an extremely rapid typist. Grandma Goldman parried with her outstanding son, Max; how he had spit in his boss's eye and a year later not only had his own business, but had paid back all the money he'd borrowed to start it, with interest; and how now, though merely twenty-five, he had made a fortune and taken his younger brothers into the business and was paying for this little vacation for his mother's health, the first in her entire life. Then a light came into the eyes of both women and they smiled at each other, not having to say another word except to exchange addresses.

It was Grandma's turn again. She told how she came to New York and ran a sewing machine in a factory, making two and a half dollars a week because she was so skilled and also because she worked about seventy-two hours a week. In her spare time, which was Sunday, if she had the strength to drag herself out of bed, the men used to look admiringly at her because she was so handsome as well as such a good worker. So it came to pass that a shadkin began coming around in order to describe his male clients to her.

"You know what's a *shadkin?*" she said to Miss Hugo, who didn't. "A marriage broker, a professional man. If he made a marriage you paid him a fee, otherwise not." Grandma only half listened to the shadkin, but one day he described a client in such glowing terms that she said all right, let him come. He did and it was a collision. The shadkin got his fee.

"He died before David was born," she said. She looked at

58

David and me with pity. "A shame you never knew him, such a wonderful man. A sense of humor he had, and such stories he told, . . . such a disposition, . . . and strong and handsome with dark brown eyes, almost black, . . . and so wise, he knew everything." Her face glowed, remembering. You could see she had really loved him. "Isn't it true, Tess?" she said, turning to my mother, whose eyes had filled with tears, as they always did when her father was mentioned.

"There was nobody like him," she said, her voice quavering. Dr. Dendritch gave her a long, intense look.

Meanwhile, I thought how similar my father's and my grandmother's stories were: two independent people who threw up everything to escape arranged marriages and then had gone ahead and married someone provided by either their mother or a shadkin. I pointed this out.

"But they didn't *force* the marriages," Dr. Dendritch explained, glad to find himself with something to say. "They merely arranged the introductions. The choice was still left to your father and grandmother."

"But not to me, really," my mother said, and told her side of the story, which was different from my father's although it was the same marriage.

"I was engaged to someone else," my mother said, astounding me.

"Some engaged!" Grandma said.

"We were going to be married," my mother said. "I didn't have the ring yet. He couldn't afford one. He was just starting out."

"A junior account," Grandma snorted. "Not even a full-fledged."

"He was working and finishing school. In another year he'd have been a CPA."

"What was he like?" I said, thrilled. "What was his name?"

"His name was Robert and he was gentle, quiet and thoughtful." I glanced at my father, who was none of these things. He wasn't in the least put out. "My father was dying then. Before he died, he wanted to see me married to someone he thought would make me happy and who would be able to give me all the things my father thought I needed. 'Marry Max,' he said to me. 'You're a girl with a strong will and Max is bashful and looks up to you, and you'll get your own way with him. Besides, he's already established, already proved himself.' I adored my father and I respected his judgment. And I wanted to make him happy before he died. So Max and I were married in the bedroom where he lay dying."

There was a long silence. It was one of the saddest stories I had ever heard because the minute they were married my father stopped being bashful and my mother stopped having a strong will.

Dinner was over then. Miss Hugo said her leg felt better so the grown-ups went into the living room and turned on the Stromberg Carlson; my father danced with Miss Hugo and my mother danced with Dr. Dendritch. I went up to my room and closed the door, and thought about my mother for the first time as a tragic figure in her own story instead of merely as the mother in mine. It made her seem like another person entirely, almost a stranger. Then, to be fair, I forced myself to think about my father that way, as a separate person, and I found that I liked *him* better in his own life than in mine.

Also, I couldn't help comparing him to Dr. Dendritch. There was no question that Dr. Dendritch was an educated, thoughtful, civilized man, but alongside my father he seemed pale and colorless and, in some way that I couldn't put my finger on, false. Still, my mother's faith in him seemed tenacious, and beginning that week, Arthur began driving David to see him every Friday after school. I couldn't wait for him to get back that first Friday.

"What did he say?" I asked when he did.

David shrugged. I followed him into the living room where he was making a beeline for the piano.

"Did he talk about your sleepwalking?"

"No. Why should he?"

"What *did* you talk about?"

"We didn't talk much. He showed me his stamp collection."

"What did he do that for?"

"How should I know."

"Was that all?"

"He gave me an envelope full of old foreign stamps."

"What for?"

"To start my collection. I'm supposed to get an album and hinges and paste them in."

"He wants you to collect stamps?" I said. But David had begun to practice and was no longer thinking about anything else.

The following week he came home clutching two little pencil drawings, which he showed my mother that night at her request.

"David," she exclaimed, "did you really do these all yourself?" David was a little too old for that kind of talk so he merely made a small mumbling noise and gazed at the ceiling. "They're just beautiful, David," my mother went on. I looked at the drawings. One was a drawing of a roller skate and the other was of a bat and ball. You could recognize what they were, but I couldn't see what all the fuss was about. "I knew you had lots of talents, David, but I didn't know drawing was one of them," my mother said in tones honeyed with admiration and awe, a woman who has just discovered that she has given birth to Michelangelo. I was annoyed.

"What's so great about them?"

"Look at the *shading,* Allegra," she said. I looked at the shading. You could see that David had worked carefully on the drawings. He had drawn these sporting goods with their shadows in front of them, as though the sun was behind them. "It's so lifelike," my mother persisted. "May I have these, David? I'd like to keep them."

She kept them. She put them in the corner of her top bureau drawer where she had a little heap of treasures. She had never asked to keep any of my drawings, which were more complicated, entire scenes filled with detail and nature in the background. Wasn't it enough that David was musical? And older? And a boy? I went to my room to think about why this episode made me feel so terrible. After I thought for a while, it came to me that it was all part of the plan to give David self-confidence and that my mother may have gotten certain instructions from Dr. Dendritch. But how come, even though I didn't walk in my sleep, no one was worried about my self-confidence? Did they think I was a tower of strength? Was it part of the plan to throw me to the wolves?

There wasn't a move David made that didn't bring a veritable avalanche of praise tumbling down on him. The most ordinary things. Ninety-two on an arithmetic test. The way he put varnish on a bookshelf made in shop. Being able to stand on ice skates without falling down. His neatness in pasting stamps in the album and his astuteness at knowing that Helvetia was Switzerland. It was sickening.

Alas, David responded. He began to act superior. He had only me to be superior to.

"Better let me do that," he said one day while I was making some smokestacks to go on top of one of his ships. "You'll only mess it up." That sort of thing. But one day he went too far.

"Everyone knows Ouagadougou is the capital of Upper Volta, stupid," he said. I hadn't even asked him; he had initiated the whole thing. "I bet you don't even know the capital of Upper Volta," he had said. I had never heard of Upper Volta. It didn't sound like a place to me. If anyone had said what's an upper volta, I'd have guessed it was part of a radio.

"They're ruining you," I said. "I'm surprised you can't see through the whole thing."

But I knew there was no use talking to him. He *liked* what they were doing to him.

One Friday he went off with a small suitcase. He was going to spend an entire weekend at Dr. Dendritch's country place in Vermont. It was a big step for a nervous sleeper who had never spent a night away from home without his family. He came back with a snapshot of himself standing in the crotch of a tree. It was a funny pose; he was wearing knickers, his good tweed overcoat with matching cap and his ordinary brown oxfords. Not even sneakers. He even had his glasses on. He was standing there with one hand resting against the tree trunk, a mysterious, self-conscious little smile on his face, not unlike the Mona Lisa or the Cheshire cat. I couldn't help guessing that Dr. Dendritch had simply lifted David up and placed him there in the tree and then stepped back to snap his picture. About the last thing in the world that David would have thought of doing would have been to climb a tree.

"How rough-and-tumble," I said, handing the picture back to him, but I knew it was going to be another treasure for my mother's dresser drawer.

63

"You're ruining David," I said to my mother soon afterwards. It was one of those rare times when she was actually sitting down in a chair in the living room, nowhere near the telephone. She was threading a needle. David was downstairs in the basement trying out a chinning bar that had been installed there so he could develop some muscles. "I mean, I think I know what you're trying to do, but you're doing it all wrong."

"What are you talking about?"

"All that telling him how marvellous he is. It's part of a plot to get him to stop spending so much time playing the piano and go outside to play ball with Spunk and Miff and Lincoln, isn't it?"

"David has an inferiority complex," my mother reminded me. "He needs to know that there are many things he can do as well as anyone, and some he can do better. He's too timid."

"I think you're overdoing it," I said. "Out there in the real world just who do you think is going to fall down in a swoon because he knows how to load a camera? I mean, *really.*"

"Why don't you just mind your own business?"

"It *is* my business. It's getting so he's impossible to live with. Besides, knowing the capital of Upper Volta isn't going to help him with the kids on the block. If he pulled some of that stuff on them, they'd knock him down."

My mother sighed and fitted a darning egg into a sock. This was uncharacteristic for someone with such limited domestic tendencies, but sock darning was one thing she had learned to do and did. I think it soothed her, and it was a defense against my father's occasional accusations that she wasn't holding up her end.

"Why can't you just tell him he's good at the things he's

64

really good at?" I said. "Instead of going all to pieces every time he names a capital?"

"We have to help him find himself."

Those phrases!

"What about the piano?" I said.

"Oh, the piano!"

"What's the matter with that?"

"What's he going to do with it?"

"Be a pianist."

"You can't just be a pianist," my mother said.

"What about all those people who play the piano in Carnegie Hall and on the radio and records? They're pianists. What about Paderewski?"

"David isn't Paderewski."

I was beginning to see a glimmer of light.

"You mean we have to help David find himself *your* way. You want him to be like everybody else. That's what you mean by finding himself, right?"

"David has to grow up to take his place in the world. I want him to be able to do that. And to be happy."

"Furthermore, how come nobody around here is at all interested in whether *I* am finding *my*self?"

"Oh, you," my mother said. "You'll grow up and marry some nice man and have children. David is a boy."

Chapter 6

Everyone was always saying how precocious I was, though they never said it as though it were anything good to be. Still, I didn't really hear about sex until the summer when I was almost nine. I knew about parts of the body, and about babies coming out of them, but I had pushed away all of the "how" questions, perhaps because I sensed that I wouldn't be ready for the answers. Naturally, I couldn't help suspecting that there was something afoot. After all, I read books. And my father, in his mellower moods, when he was being his idea of jolly, was not above making certain innuendoes in mixed company, at which my mother would usually veil her eyes and feign a yawn.

It took my cousin Sonia to deliver me from ignorance. My cousin Sonia was my age but an entirely different type, so that although we saw a lot of each other, we never really became friends. Sonia was shorter than I and more feminine, with a pile of gold hair and a nose that wrinkled when she smiled.

I mean it deliberately wrinkled. Sonia was making a career of being cute. She was bright but not particularly intelligent, and our interests couldn't have been more dissimilar.

"They call it intercause," she said.

We were at Zimmerman's Silver Birch Colony, a family-type summer resort on a big lake in Sullivan County, New York. We were there for the whole summer: our family, two sets of aunts and uncles, and three of my mother's buddies: Jennie, Ann and Ethel, with their broods. Our crowd filled half the place, so my mother had a game every minute, though she did find time for nine holes of golf every day and a swim afterwards.

"Intercause?" I said. "Don't be silly. I'd have heard of it."

I had never gotten anything good from my cousin Sonia. I had gotten whooping cough from her, and measles, and a certain amount of jealousy, but that was it.

"Anyhow," I said, "who would do anything like that?"

"Everyone," Sonia said. She was being a ballerina that summer. At this point she rose up on her toes and pirouetted pretty badly, arcing her arms up over her head, a bower to tippy-toe under. She had short, plump arms.

"Men and women everywhere / In and out of doors / Morning noon and evening / Are doing intercause," she sang as she danced.

I was getting angry.

"My parents wouldn't do anything as dumb as that," I said.

"Ha, ha," she said darkly. "Your parents *especially.*"

I punched her in the mouth. She looked surprised, then burst into tears and turned and ran. I proceeded on down to the lake where I had been headed in the first place. I was meeting David there. We were going to fish off the dock. I had gone for the drop lines while he rounded up the bait.

"What took you so long?" he said when I got there. He was sitting on the end of the dock, his skinny legs dangling off it. Though we hadn't been at Zimmerman's Silver Birch Colony very long, we were already sunburned and David's nose was peeling.

"Nothing. That pest Sonia," I said.

He had a can of worms. I had never fished before and I didn't see how I was going to be able to thread a live worm onto the hook. I watched David do it and it made me sick.

"I don't think I can do that," I said.

"They don't feel anything," he said with contempt.

"How do you know? Look how it's squirming."

"I read it. See, it doesn't even bleed."

"Are you telling me that things that don't bleed have no feelings?"

"Very little," he said. "Don't you know that if you cut a worm in half both parts will grow new ends and you'll have two worms?"

He was a mine of information. I wondered if he knew anything about sex.

"You do it for me," I said.

"If you're going to fish you have to be able to bait your own hook."

I steeled myself and reached for a worm. Then, with my eyes closed, I hung it onto the hook through its middle. It was the best I could do and that was bad enough.

"You'll never catch a fish with that," David said. "He'll just take it right off the hook."

I lowered it anyway and sat there waiting.

"Sonia just told me a really dumb thing," I said.

"You're not supposed to talk when you're fishing. The fish will hear you. What did she tell you?"

"She's crazy, Sonia. She called it The Facts of Life."

"Oh, that."

I looked at David, stunned. "You know about it?" I said.

"Naturally."

"It's true?"

"How do you think babies get made?"

"But Sonia says people do it anyway, even when they're not making babies. She says they *like* it."

"Yeah."

"Why would they like something like that?"

"They have to like it. I mean, think about it. If they didn't like it, why would they ever do it? And if they didn't do it how would anybody ever get born? Actually, they love it. They even *call* it love."

"*That*'s not what love is," I said.

"It's one kind of love. It's carnal love."

"What's carnal?"

"Carnal means meat. Chili con carne. That's chili with meat."

"Oh, for Pete's sake, David!"

"Well, flesh, then. It's fleshy love."

At that moment something jerked my line, and I was so surprised I almost fell into the lake.

"I think I've got something," I screamed.

"Pull it up," David screamed. "Quick. Don't let it get away."

I pulled it up and threw it onto the dock. It was a fat little fish, all gold and silver in the sun. It looked like one of my mother's beaded evening bags flopping around there, except that it had an eye and that eye was staring at me. I looked away.

"I think I'll throw it back," I said.

69

"What do you want to do a dumb thing like that for?" David yelled. "When you're fishing and you catch a fish you're supposed to keep the fish, that's what it's all about."

"I don't care what it's all about. I'm going to throw it back. Take the hook out, will you?"

"Take it out yourself."

The fish was no longer flopping around. It was gasping. I knelt down warily and took hold of the line as near the fish's mouth as I dared. I couldn't see the hook anywhere. Tentatively, I tugged at the line and the fish gave a leap and so did I.

"It's stuck," I said.

"Naturally it's stuck. It's supposed to be stuck."

"Stop always telling me how things are supposed to be and come get this hook out of this fish," I hollered, very near hysteria. David came and held the fish with one hand and worked the line with the other.

"It won't come out," he said. "He swallowed the hook."

I looked at the fish and the fish looked at me. I don't know how long we looked at each other, but then I saw something I had never seen before. I saw the life go out of the fish's eye. One minute that eye had life in it and then it was gone. It was my first sight of death. I had seen dead things lots of times, in the fish market and the butcher shop, but this was my first encounter with actual dying.

I sat down on the dock and looked at the fish. As I looked, I could see the fish's scales gradually grow duller and duller. It went on happening. I looked at my hands that had done this thing. My own hands. Meanwhile, David's hands were tugging at the line and it was beginning to give. He had one sneakered foot on the fish's tail, pinning it to the dock. Suddenly the line came free, bringing with it not only the hook, but what must have been all that fish's insides, right through the fish's mouth. There was a lot of blood, too.

"That fish had blood," I said, and then I threw up my breakfast into the lake.

I left David and went to the swimming dock. Vic, the lifeguard, was alone there. He sat tilted back in a canvas chair, zinc ointment on his nose, his eyes hidden behind purple sunglasses.

"Hi," I said. When he didn't answer, I realized he was asleep. I sat down at the edge of the dock and looked at the brownish water, still feeling sick. The sun was strong on me and it felt good. I sat for a while, hoping it would burn away the poisons, and I looked at Vic. His skin was a good red-bronze color, and the hair on his muscled legs and forearms glinted gold in the sunlight. I looked at the flat planes of his chest and then at the enormous bulge in his swimming trunks. Then I saw Mrs. Paradise clumping towards the dock on flapping mules with heels about six inches high. I watched the way her hips and breasts swayed as she walked, thinking what a waste all that sideways motion was when you were going forward. Mrs. Paradise was about my mother's age, but my mother didn't like her. I had overheard snatches of conversation about her. Her husband had given her some money "to play with," whatever that meant, and she had run it up into "quite a little pile," and ever since then her husband had been afraid of her.

She came onto the dock and spread her towel next to the chair where Vic sat.

"Good morning, lover," she said. Vic came awake sluggishly, like a turtle.

"Oh, there you are," he said.

"Be a doll and rub some of this stuff on my back," Mrs.

Paradise said, handing Vic a tube of suntan cream. She spread herself onto her towel, stomach down. There was a lot of her, most of it flesh, and most of that flesh concentrated in her chest and thighs and behind. She was carnal. I wondered how it felt, carrying all that around.

Vic hunkered down next to her and began to spread cream on her back, rubbing it in slow circles.

"Ooh, that feels good," Mrs. Paradise purred.

"Slept pretty late today for some reason, didn't you?" Vic said. "I didn't see you at breakfast."

"I wonder why," she said and then gave a funny laugh that wasn't a laugh. "Ooh, don't stop. You can do the backs of my legs now."

I was beginning to feel uncomfortable watching them, so I looked away. I looked down at my own body. I was wearing a pair of old green wool swimming shorts outgrown by David. Except at meals, they were practically all I had worn every day since we had gotten to Zimmerman's. I looked at the scab on my left knee and then I looked at my legs. They were perfectly straight legs, getting longer every minute. Arms, too. There were no hidden mysteries in my body. There were the bones, maybe an eighth of an inch of carne over that and then the skin. That was all. Functional, the way a body ought to be. Of course, there were the private parts, but there wasn't much to them, either, and besides I was sitting on those, which, except for going to the bathroom, was mainly what they were for. Whereas Vic's and Mrs. Paradise's private parts seemed much more public. I looked down at my chest. It was perfectly flat, no different from David's, and I meant to keep it that way.

Then, all at once, something in the day tilted, I don't know why, and I found that I was acutely aware of my nakedness and burning with shame, the feeling I'd had once or twice in dreams when I was at the Paramount Theater among thousands of people and I hadn't a stitch on except for my saddle shoes. Although Mrs. Paradise and Vic were the only people there, and they were as aware of me as they were of the dragonfly that swooped across my toes and began skimming the lake's surface in search of lunch, I felt so brazenly exposed that the only thing to do was to slide into the water and hide my nakedness. I paddled around for a while, treading water, watching the dragonfly and praying for an eclipse so that I could steal out in darkness back to our cabin and my clothes. A second dragonfly came along and settled on the back of the first one. The bottom dragonfly didn't seem to mind; it just went on about its business with the other one in tandem, their wings a lovely geometry of stained-glass windows.

I don't know how long I stayed in the water. The skin of my fingers had puckered to prune skin when I told myself that sooner or later I was going to have to come out of there and that the longer I waited the more people there were apt to be about. I swam around to the ladder furthest from Vic and Mrs. Paradise and, telling myself that I was a merchild and that they were ungifted with sight for fabled creatures and therefore blind to me, I came silently dripping up onto the dock, where I broke into a run. I ran all the way up the hill, past the dining hall and the social hall and around behind the tennis courts, and didn't stop until I was safely inside our cabin. I went straight into my mother's room. She was taking a nap. I stood at the foot of her bed for a while, looking at the soles of her feet. "Those are the soles of the feet of my own mother," I told myself, trying not to feel so angry with her.

I went to the mirror over her bureau and looked at my face. I had never thought much about my face, but now I wanted to see what sort of face it was and how much of a chance I was going to have in the world with it, and I couldn't see it. I could see this collection of eyes and nose and mouth and straight, tangled, wet hair, but I couldn't tell a thing about my face. It was so familiar to me that it had become the face of a stranger.

My mother stirred. In the mirror, I saw her eyes flutter open.

"What would you say my best feature was?" I said.

"Your eyes," she said, yawning.

"Why my eyes? Why not my nose or my mouth?"

"Because your eyes are so big and blue and they're what people see first. Bring me my cigarettes, puss."

I scooped them off the top of the bureau and brought them to her.

"I'm ordinary-looking though, aren't I?"

"You'll turn out all right," she said, humoring me. My anger came back then.

"You let me run around looking like this," I said.

"Looking like what?"

"Without even a real bathing suit with a top and a bottom."

"I thought you liked those drawers."

"I never even thought about them before," I yelled.

"Did you catch any fish?"

"I don't want to discuss that. What about this bathing suit, that's what I'm thinking about now."

"I'll go into town and buy you a bathing suit this afternoon. You want to go with me?"

"No. Just make sure it's a *real* bathing suit. I'm sick and tired of being the bottom rung of the ladder around here. All the guts came out of the fish through its mouth. I don't see why we have to have that pest Sonia here all summer ruining everything."

I stormed into my room and changed into a pair of regular

74

shorts and a shirt and stormed on out, banging the screen door behind me. I felt like doing something difficult, so I headed for the tennis courts, thinking that if Herman, the tennis pro, was too busy to give me a lesson, I could just smash some balls around. There weren't many men at Zimmerman's during the week, as the fathers and husbands came out only for weekends. Just the staff and Mr. Rothman, a semi-invalid with a cane, and his son Jerry, a tall, sallow, seventeen-year-old on whose arm Mr. Rothman leaned when he had to navigate. I had to pass Mr. Rothman on my way to the tennis courts, as he was seated on a bench built around the trunk of a beech tree just off the path. Mr. Rothman was one of the few adults around who bothered to speak to children. He always had a pocket full of candy, and it was impossible to pass him without being offered some.

"Would you like some licorice, Allegra?" he asked. I don't like licorice but I did like Mr. Rothman. He had nice creases in his cheeks and a soft pleasant voice and a lot of dignity. I sat down next to him and thanked him for the licorice.

"Isn't it a beautiful day," he said. "I never cease to wonder at the sky here. I suppose that's because I never really get to see it on West Ninety-Third Street."

"Mr. Rothman," I said, "very few grownups ever bother to talk to children. Is it because they don't really think we're people?"

"Yes," he said.

I sucked on the long braid of licorice, tasting the black.

"Mr. Rothman," I said, "every day life gets harder and harder. Does that ever stop?"

"No," he said.

I took my leave. Herman was finishing a lesson with a pretty teenager named Dolores. I sat down and watched, still sucking the licorice. Herman was a wizard tennis player and my favorite of all the men on the staff. Before dinner most nights, and sometimes after it, too, a group of the staff men sat around with my mother and her cronies outside the social hall, talking and having cocktails. I could tell Herman was partial to my mother, even though she was thirty-two that summer, much older than Herman, who was still in graduate school studying to be a research physicist. Sometimes they even took walks together. I liked him anyway. Though not especially handsome, he had a vocabulary, and that interested me. I was beginning to realize that when you know a lot you need a larger and larger vocabulary so that you know that you know it.

"Greetings," Herman called. A ball had rolled to the side of the court where I was sitting and he came to get it. "You look in fine fettle today."

Fettle.

"I'm feeling a bit poorly today, Herman."

"I'm sorry to hear that. Perhaps we can find a remedy."

He went back to lob a few more balls to Dolores's backhand. For some reason I was glad to see that she missed most of them. She was pretty in her sparkling little white getup, but she was a lousy tennis player.

"Enough!" she cried, finally. "I'm worn out."

I watched them converge, winding up the lesson with a flurry of animated conversation. Dolores was one of those people who can't talk to anyone without touching them. I watched her hand dart back and forth, first to clutch one of Herman's hands, then a bicep, back to the hand, then a shoulder pat. She smiled radiantly all the while, her eyelashes flapping. I knew I would never in my life be able to act that way.

"Are you in love with Dolores?" I said when the latter had finally departed.

"Good lord, no," Herman said, laughing. "You want to play some tennis?"

"Are you in love with anyone?"

"Not at the moment. Why do you ask?"

"Were you ever in love with anyone?"

"Yes."

"How did it feel?"

He didn't answer right away. He had to think about it, I noticed.

"It feels like different things at different times," he said. "Why? Do you think you might be in love?"

"Don't be silly. If I were I'd know how it feels, wouldn't I?"

"Do you want to work on your serve?"

"When people love someone very much," I said, "why would they want to do intercause with them?"

Herman made a face. "Intercourse," he said. "That's a clinical term. When two people love each other they want to be very, very close. And that's something special and beautiful."

I looked hard at Herman to see if he was telling the truth. He was.

"But there's more to it than that, isn't there?" I said, thinking of Mrs. Paradise and Vic. "People do intercourse—"

"Have intercourse."

"—have intercourse even when they don't love each other, don't they?"

"Yes," Herman said after a pause. "In the way that people who enjoy food sometimes eat when they aren't particularly hungry. Making love when you aren't in love is different from making love when you are, but it can still be very nice."

The subject was more complicated than I had imagined. I was getting tired of it.

"Let's work on my serve," I said.

That night during dinner Mr. Rothman had some kind of fit on the dining room floor.

We had already finished the appetizer and the soup and were about midway through the stuffed breast of veal with mashed potatoes and carrots and peas when there was a strange loud wail, an animal sound, and everyone stopped what they were doing and saying and turned, in the sudden silence, toward where the sound had come from. And it was Mr. Rothman. He was on the floor, writhing and twitching and jerking, his tongue flapping around, and I never saw anything worse. His son Jerry jumped up and knelt beside him and stuffed a napkin into his mouth. I was sitting next to Sonia, who began to giggle. She always giggled when she didn't know what else to do. It never occurred to her that she could be silent and not do anything. I could have killed her, although I am sorry to say that instead of just feeling sorry for poor Mr. Rothman, I was frightened to death. I was so frightened that I had to get up and run out of the dining room. I ran all the way down to the lake where the sun was setting, huge and orange, all fire.

I sat down and watched the sun and thought about poor Mr. Rothman writhing there on the floor as though devils had gotten inside him. I had thought and asked a lot of questions that day, but the most important thing I learned had come in those moments of silence, for I knew then that people's bodies will do what they have to do without their owner's having anything to say about it, and that my own body would change, in spite of me, and get fleshier and fleshier, and I was going to have to grow up and be a woman. And I was even going to die. It was all there in my own body. I looked at the palm of my hand, my own hand, and saw the rotting that was written there, and the skeleton waiting inside. It was certain; only time stood between me and it. And there was nothing, absolutely nothing, that anyone in the world could tell me that would change it. I felt lonelier than I had ever felt in my life.

David came down to the lake, looking for me.

"Mom was worried about you," he said. "Are you okay?"

I started to cry. I felt too tired and confused to do anything else. David sat down next to me and waited, looking embarrassed.

"What are you crying for?" he said, finally.

"I don't know," I said. "Don't you ever cry?" It had been years since I remembered seeing him cry.

"Boys don't cry."

"What's so great about that?"

"Babies cry. Babies and girls."

"What's wrong with crying when you feel like it?" I said. "You laugh when you feel like it. David, if you really felt like crying, *could* you?"

"I doubt it," he said.

Chapter 7

"Oh, God," I said, "is there no end?"

My mother had just finished telling me about menstruation. When, toward the end of that summer, she noticed that although I was eating with my usual enormous appetite, I was nonetheless losing weight, she had the staff physician examine me. He did the customary things and then he asked me if I saw spots before my eyes.

"What sort of spots?" I asked.

"Just little dots floating about. That aren't really there."

"What color?"

"Black."

"Like periods?"

Free-floating phantom punctuation. I wondered what you would have to have wrong with you to be granted such a vision. But the doctor refused to go on with this dialogue, having inferred from my questions that the answer to his was no. After a while, he shrugged and mumbled something to my mother about puberty, or maybe it was prepuberty, and told her not to worry. I didn't want to mention that I threw up every night, because I felt that if it was out in the open, all sorts of things would be confirmed that would only make everything even blacker than it already was. I might as well have mentioned it, though, because things got blacker anyhow. My mother felt it was time I knew The Facts of Life.

"I already know all about that," I said, "and I'd rather not discuss it."

My mother looked surprised and also relieved.

"Do you know about menstruation?" she asked.

"No. What *is* men's truation?" I said, resigning myself. So she told me, and it was even worse than anything I could have made up. I had to admit that mechanically it was pretty ingenious, even if it did confirm the growing knowledge of the surprises my body was saving up for me. Actually, it was years before I would have to start coping will all those eggs, so I can't imagine why my mother felt that I needed so much advance notice. I had already had more than enough for one summer. For a while I thought about getting it all over with there and then. I could outwit my body by putting an end to it. Once, in the lake, I even sort of tried. I stopped swimming, let myself sink and looked at everything that was going on in the water, which was quite a lot, much to my surprise, but pretty soon I just bobbed up again like a cork. It isn't easy to drown.

One night I was lying in bed trying to fall asleep before the nausea peaked and telling myself Tiger tiger burning bright in the forests of the night I walk along the street of sorrow the boulevard of broken dreams where if I had the wings of an angel *geb cocken offen yom* found a million-dollar baby in the five-and-ten-cent store, to keep from remembering dying or whatever it was that I was so terrified of and the nausea peaked anyway. I was cold and tired and it was a dark night and I couldn't make it to the bathroom, so I threw up in a wastepaper basket that was next to the bed. And that was how my mother found out.

"Oh, I do it every night," I said in an offhand way. I was beginning to have an idea that there was one thing she could say that might save me.

"Why?" She was horrified.

"I think it's from fear," I said, deciding to risk all.

"Fear of what?"

"Dying," I said. "My own dying. I keep thinking about it. I can't help it." Now was the time for her to say, Of course, everyone goes through that, it's a phase, it will pass. And then, knowing there would be an end to it, I would be saved.

"But you have your whole life ahead of you," she argued. "It's years and years and years before you have to begin thinking about that."

"Isn't it something everyone goes through?" I said, desperately cueing her. "Isn't it just an ordinary, natural, normal, common thing?"

"Of course not," she said, dooming me. "It's just your wild imagination."

Soon after that the summer was over and we were back in the city. One Saturday night just before school was to start, we were given a real treat: dinner out with our parents and then a movie at the Loew's Kings. At *night.* Dinner was at a Chinese restaurant on Flatbush Avenue. Either Chinese restaurants were just coming into vogue, or my parents had just found out about them, but there was still a certain amount of dark suspicion about Chinese food, just as there was about Chinese people. Too exotic. Until that night, whenever we had gone with our parents to a Chinese restaurant, David and I had only been allowed to have a taste of the Chinese food they were eating while we had bacon and tomato sandwiches on toast with mayonnaise. Bacon and tomato sandwiches were a treat for us, too, at that time, bacon being a forbidden food because Grandma, who was kosher, lived with us. But that night we were allowed to have egg-drop soup and egg rolls and chow mein and fried rice. I thought Chinese food was about the best thing in the world.

So I was feeling pretty happy when we got to the Loew's Kings and started to watch the movie. Also, there was something sinful about going to the movies at night, although years later the reverse would be true and an afternoon movie would seem sinful to me. Because the theater was too crowded for us to get four seats together, David and I sat a few rows from our parents. It was a scary movie. This lady was going to be murdered at the stroke of midnight on this particular Friday night, but no one knew who was going to do it or how. So the lady decided to have a big party that night and all her friends came dressed in evening clothes, and drank champagne and ate canapés, and as the evening wore on they got more and more nervous, especially the lady who was to be murdered. When it got close to midnight, everyone formed a protective circle around the lady, who was standing in the middle of the living room. The camera focused first on everyone in the circle (because there was no way of knowing which, if any, of them was the villain), and then on everything in the room, including the chandelier (because there was no way of knowing what it was that might be rigged to do the lady in), and everyone kept watching the clock. It was a big grandfather clock; we had been shown a lot of it so that we could tell how close we were getting to the fatal hour. I began to shiver; I was suddenly colder than I had ever been.

"It's only a movie," David said, because he could feel my seat jiggling. "It's only a shadow on a screen."

It was the kind of clock where a door opened on the hour, and when, at the stroke of twelve, it did, a deadly scorpion came out and made straight for the lady. I don't know if it killed her or not, and I certainly never found out how the scorpion knew it was midnight and which lady to strike, because by then I was unconscious. The next thing I knew we were in the car and everything was blurry and freezing cold. I heard my mother tell my father that it was probably the chow mein and to hurry because I was burning up, and I tried to tell her that on the contrary I was freezing to death, but it was too much trouble.

Afterwards, there was a time when I knew I was in my own bed. It was very comfortable there. I floated in and out of the deepest sleep I'd ever known. Once I was aware of Grandma putting something cool on my head, once of Dr. Wise standing at the foot of the bed looking grave and once I smelled rubbing alcohol, but mostly it was a dream I floated in and out of, feeling as mindless and as vaporous as a cloud. And there was darkness: a soft, furry dark with an occasional hazy pinpoint of golden light somewhere off in the distance.

And no fear.

When I awoke, finally, to full daylight, and all the things in my room were there, back in focus, Grandma was sitting next to the bed putting a fresh cool washcloth on my forehead. I felt exhausted and weak, as though I had just come home from a grueling trip across a desert, or an arctic waste, or both, so I looked at Grandma to make sure.

"Am I sick?" I said. Her face lit up, though her eyes filled with tears.

"Ketzelah, ketzelah," she said (that means pussycat, pussycat), kissing and hugging me. She got out a handkerchief and blew her nose. "Three days you lay in a coma."

"What's a coma?" I said.

"Unconscious. Wait, let me run get Mama, she's taking a little nap."

It was pneumonia, but the crisis was past. The crisis was when you either died or didn't. I didn't. But to have a crisis you have to nearly die. I had nearly died. If I had died then I wouldn't even have known it. Or minded. It was something to think about, and in the days that followed I did. A lot. Sir Alexander Fleming hadn't come up with penicillin yet, much less with being a Sir, so I had to stay in bed for a long time recuperating and avoiding a relapse. Two new words for me, both beginning with *re.* I stayed in bed one month, not even getting out of it to go to the bathroom. It was an interesting month.

For one thing, everyone seemed pleased that I hadn't died, even my father. When he came home that first evening after the crisis, he came upstairs right away to see me.

"Well," he said, sitting down heavily on the edge of the bed, "you gave us a pretty bad scare. Don't ever do that again."

"I didn't do it on purpose," I said. No more, I thought, than Mr. Rothman had his fit on the dining room floor on purpose. No more than I chose being born a girl, etc. But right then I was feeling too pleased to go into all that. I was even glad that my father was my father.

"You're going to have to stay in bed now for a few weeks and take very good care of yourself. I want you to promise me that you'll do everything your mother and the doctor tell you and no monkey business."

"Sure," I said.

"And I'm going to get you a present. What do you want most in the world?"

"A bicycle."

"You can't have a bicycle."

"How about a saxophone?" I said.

"You can't have a saxophone. Girls don't play saxophones."

"What about Phil Spitalney and his all-girl orchestra?"

"Think of something else," he said.

"How many things do you think there are that I want most in the world?" I said.

"What about a doll?" he said.

There was a time when dolls were all they ever gave me for birthdays, and I always cried when they did, it made me so angry.

"Oh, Daddy," I said, "I'm too old for dolls. I'll think it over and let you know when I come up with something."

Another good thing was not having to go to school. At one point my mother went to see my teacher to get the books we were using that term, but all she came back with was a nice note from Miss Roach telling me not to think about school or anything else but getting completely well and that I would have no trouble catching up with the class when the time came.

The best thing, though, was that I had a little silver bell next to the bed, and every time I rang it someone came running upstairs to my room to see what I wanted.

Power. My magic lantern. But unlike magic, or everything in fairy tales, there were no threes about my bell; it was unlimited. In the first week I slept a lot, so even without my having to ring someone was always there plying me with nourishment or medicine. But as I began to feel better, I also grew increasingly bored and restless and the bell tinkled more and more often.

"Have mercy," my mother finally said one day. She was beginning to look a bit haggard.

"I need some more books," I said. "Can you go to the library today?"

"Yes. Anything special?"

I had run through all of Albert Payson Terhune and Zane Grey and Louisa May Alcott.

"No more dogs or sagebrush," I said.

"What about adventure? Jungles? The sea?"

"I don't think so," I said. "Try the grown-up section. Ask the librarian."

She did, and for some reason she came back with a stack of Englishmen: Hugh Walpole, H. G. Wells, Galsworthy, Maugham. A whole new world. The bell rang only when my stomach or some other organ insisted. I was rapt. I was learning the following:

1. Some people talked much better than we did.

2. Money was not the most important thing in the world.

3. People had different ideas about the meaning of life and they gave it a lot of thought.

4. People needed some center to their lives, some driving force, some system of order, as well as a code.

5. I was not the only one concerned with death; in fact, we were all in this together.

6. Writers had more to tell than just stories. Even in stories.

Just thinking about that whole library filled with ideas, things to mull over, all sorts of new people to get to know, boggled my mind. I had so much to think about. Something in one of the books started me thinking about souls. The soul. Naturally, this had come up before. When you died your soul went to heaven. When I stopped believing in Santa Claus, and in ghosts, which was almost at once, I stopped believing in heaven. What would they need a heaven for if there were no such things as ghosts or elves or fairies, etcetera? Weren't souls in the same category? Insofar as you could describe our family as having any philosophy at all, we were rationalists. Materialistic rationalists. Or possibly rationalistic materialists, but without much consciousness. My parents professed to believe in God, but I rarely heard his name mentioned unattached to "damn" or "sakes" or "willing." And though my parents belonged to a big temple on Ocean Avenue, they went to it only twice a year, on Rosh Hashana and Yom Kippur, and I had never set foot in it at all, being a girl. My brother would be bar mitzvah'd there, but the daughters of certain sorts of Jews had no need of religious training, because they weren't sons. My ignorance was total.

I asked my parents why they went to temple only twice a year and those two times within a week of each other. They said because those were the high holy days when you atoned for your sins and prayed for the dead.

"What happens on the low holy days?" I asked, but the answer was vague, something about ordinary services except on special holidays, and that it was really a sin to miss R. H. and Y. K. I then wanted to know, if all you had to do to atone for your sins and honor your dead was attend two services a year, why would anyone bother to go at any other time, and the answer was that some people were more religious than

88

others, especially the elderly. Naturally, I wanted to know how my parents had decided just how much religion was enough, but they didn't seem to know the answer to this and changed the subject.

Grandma considered herself religious. Orthodox, she said, but not as orthodox as some. She didn't wear a wig, or anything like that, but we had two sets of dishes and cutlery and dish towels and Rokeach soap for the dishes, and no part of a pig or spineless fish was allowed in the house. We couldn't mix dairy and meat at the same meal, the reason for that, Grandma said, being that it wasn't sensitive to eat the child with its mother's milk, but I wouldn't care to vouch for the accuracy of that. Most of the dietary laws, Grandma said, had evolved for reasons of health and sanitation, and while those reasons might no longer pertain, owing to refrigeration and government inspection, it was still sinful to break the laws. Reform Jews did, but not Orthodox Jews. Anyhow, the mere smell of bacon frying made Grandma sick to her stomach, so it was too late for her to change.

Grandma also lit candles Friday night and there were *Yahrzeit* candles lit for the dead, and special meals and even different kinds of cake for special holidays. Grandma and my father fasted on Yom Kippur, and dinner that night was always a huge breakfast, which both of them, starved and shriven, approached with an air of such virtue that we felt awed by their presence and spoke to them in whispers.

But the busiest religious time of the year was Passover, a happy time; winter was over and the windows were flung open to let in the early spring sunlight, the fresh April breezes and the cries of the I-Cash-Clothes man, while everything was scrubbed, the Passover dishes brought in from the garage (where they were stored the rest of the year) and the flour and bread thrown out to make way for the glossy boxes of mat-zoths, macaroons and half-gallons of sweet syrupy wine. And what a flurry of preparation for the Passover feast! What a chopping of fish and a simmering of soup and a baking of *tsimmes* and a roasting of capon and an assembling of *taigloch!* Grandma was in her element, humming Russian tunes, a beaming earth mother with her sleeves rolled up and her eyes shining. I did love Passover. And Grandma's observance of it was devout, but it was the domestic, the kitchen side of religion.

Even when it came to God, alas, the woman's place was in the kitchen.

That was the sum of my religious background when I began seriously to think about souls. I suppose if I hadn't been so needy at that time, all those casual references to the soul, to the spiritual versus the physical, and so forth, wouldn't have gotten special attention from me, as they certainly weren't central to the books I was reading. But as it happened, they jumped off the pages. Also, the authors of those books were highly intelligent men who had obviously given a great deal of thought to a variety of subjects, had unusual vocabularies and were English. It was much harder to argue with them than with Grandma and my parents, especially as what they said was in print. So one of the things I was busy with during my long recuperation was slowly coming to believe, thanks to bits and snatches of novels, that though the body was ingeniously executed, it was still only a machine (and a faulty one) to be driven by the true essence of the person, that which made him uniquely himself and not someone else: his soul, or spirit. And the soul was infinitely more complicated than the body, a much more difficult job for God, so that it couldn't be wasted at death along with the used-up body. Yes, the soul was precious and unexpendable, the true home of the individual.

What a relief. I was equipped with religion and had solved the problem of dying and most of my fears of it.

Now that I had thought all this out, I wanted to see it all written down so that I could be absolutely sure I believed it. So one night I told my father that what I wanted most in the world was a typewriter. Typed, the words might be almost as convincing as they were printed. It was a choice my father approved without reservation, as he believed I planned to begin training for a secretarial career so that in due time, if not sooner, I would be equipped to earn my first dollar. The next day, smiling proudly, he deposited it on my bed, a beautiful black Underwood portable with steel-rimmed keys, all the ribs showing and a black-and-red ribbon, the red for emphasis. It made me feel twenty-five years old.

The first thing I did was type out my religion for David, whom I had decided to proselytize. It filled two pages, double spaced, but that may have been because I used as many words as I could think of. I wanted to squeeze as many words out of my new typewriter as possible.

"David," I said, after he came home from school that day and before he had started to practice, "I want you to read this when you have the time."

"What is it?" he said, taking the pages from me and glancing at them.

"It's a religion."

"Which one?"

"My own."

He snorted, sat down on the foot of my bed and began to read. Halfway down the first page he yawned dramatically.

"This is boring," he said.

"Religions are supposed to be boring."

He read a little further. "Everybody knows about souls. You think you made that up?"

"I don't know. I just put it all together a little differently."

"What makes you think so? You don't know anything about the religions there already are. Maybe you ought to read up on those before you go inventing your own."

"You're so smart," I said. "You always know so much."

"Just because you're scared about dying you think everyone is," he said. "I'm not scared about dying."

"You're not?"

"I hardly ever even think about it," he said, handing me back my religion, which he never finished reading, and going downstairs to work on a polonaise.

The only thing that had ever frightened me was about the only thing that had never frightened David.

What a mystery it all was.

Chapter 8

"Today we are going to learn how to light the oven," Miss Botchford announced. She was a large, jolly-looking woman with a heart of stone, and she stood like a queen in the center of her gleaming white enamel stronghold, her pots and pans in neat array, her subjects, fourteen maidens in white aprons, openmouthed before her, agog at the prospect. We had already learned toast. We had learned applesauce. But once we had mastered oven lighting we could proceed to some really complicated delicacies, like melted cheese sandwiches. We could hardly wait.

How I had balked!

"Mr. Kelleher," I had said to our principal, "I came to school to improve my mind, not to learn toast and applesauce." Besides, I already knew toast.

"Sometimes, Allegra, in the course of human affairs and for the common good, it is required of us that we do something that we might not choose to do. Ours not to reason why."

"With all due respect, Mr. Kelleher, sir," I murmured, "P.S. 193 is not my nation."

"It is our purpose, as well as our hope, to prepare you children to the best of our ability to meet the demands of the world that lies ahead of you." He was a wordy man.

"How come the boys don't have to take cooking?" I said. "Name me one great chef who was a woman."

"We are not teaching you to become great chefs," Mr. Kelleher said. "You girls will grow up to be housewives and mothers, and we are preparing you for the duties and obligations you will, happily, encounter when you arrive at that state."

"All the boys around here are planning to be gynecologists or ear, nose and throat men. How come you're preparing them to be carpenters?"

"You are trying my patience, Allegra."

So there I was in my white apron. I had reported all this to my brand-new best friend, Melanie Traphagen. She was new in the neighborhood, new in the school and the first person I had ever found I could really talk to, even about the most serious things.

"If they're preparing us to be housewives and mother," Melanie said, "why don't they teach us something really useful like sexual intercourse?"

That's the kind of girl she was. Brainy.

"Now I'm going to show you how to light the oven and I want you to watch every move carefully," Miss Botchford said, and she lit the oven.

We stood there waiting for what would come next. Revelation hung in the air.

"Allegra, would you kindly come forward."

Sensing mutiny, Miss Botchford hadn't left me alone for a minute from the very first class. I stepped forward.

"Allegra, would you kindly light the oven now in the manner I just demonstrated."

I struck a match.

"No, no, Allegra. Start again."

I had failed to open the oven door first. I did this and struck another match.

"No, no, Allegra!"

I had struck the match towards me instead of away. This time, I got as far as actually turning on the gas and holding the flame to the little hole without committing a single gaffe. Triumphant, I shook out the match.

"No, no, Allegra. We *blow* out the match. You'll have to take it all over again from the beginning."

I looked at Melanie. Her face showed that she was sharing my feelings. These were mixed.

I did it all again flawlessly and chucked the match into the wastepaper basket.

"Oh, no, Allegra! That's the worst sin of all." Had I been less unlucky, you see, I might have burned down the school. So I did it again. And again. And again.

"I didn't know there was such an art to this, Miss Botchford," I said. "I want to thank you for opening my eyes."

"She was picking on you again," Melanie said later that day when, released, we were sitting on the front stoop, reviewing life. "She really likes you."

"*Likes* me!" I shrieked.

"In a strange way."

"You can say that again."

"Sadistically."

"What's that?"

"Don't you know what sadism is? To say nothing of masochism?"

"No."

Melanie sighed. It meant she was going to have to lend me another book. She was always lending me books so that I could catch up with her in her fields of special knowledge, which were many. Not that she minded lending books; it was the wasted time she minded. She liked me to be ready to discuss things with her the moment they popped into her mind. We had begun to solve this problem by reading the same books at the same time. Whichever one of us went to the library took out two of everything.

"Skip it," she said. "It's not important. What is important is that the whole system has to be overhauled."

We had already overhauled the entire political system, after a fashion, as Melanie was a Marxist. She itched to join the Abraham Lincoln Brigade to go to Spain to fight the fascist threat. I was not really terribly interested in politics. Melanie said this was because I was too neurotic to give myself to the larger issues. I didn't even know what neurotic meant. Melanie said that I of all people should have known the meaning of neurotic as I had already had one nervous breakdown. This came as a complete surprise to me and I looked at her askance. She explained that beyond a doubt that whole summer of fear and trembling and vomiting I had described to her had been nothing more nor less than a nervous breakdown, and what did I think a nervous breakdown was, anyway. I hadn't thought anything about nervous breakdowns, so was not prepared to say. But I was grateful to Melanie for giving a name to that bad time. Labeling it changed it by making it less amorphous and part of the common experience. It was comforting.

I really loved Melanie. I had never had trouble making friends but always before a friend had been someone to play with. Melanie was the first friend who was someone to *be* with.

When she first came into the class I hadn't paid much attention to her. Most of our class had been together from the time I had skipped into it from first grade. Ours was not a fluid neighborhood, most of our parents being owners rather than renters. A newcomer in the class was an event, but also an intrusion, and Melanie hadn't looked particularly promising to me at the beginning, being solemn and deceptively bland. But on the third morning I began to suspect that she was someone to be reckoned with.

"Melanie, dear," Miss Roach said (she was a kind teacher), "I notice you aren't saying the pledge of allegiance along with the rest of us. Don't you know it?"

"I know it," Melanie said.

"Aren't you a citizen of this country, dear?"

"Yes I am, Miss Roach. I was born right here in Brooklyn."

"Then don't you feel you owe this country your allegiance?"

"Some," Melanie said. "But not that much."

There was a shocked silence. This sort of thing was unheard of back then, at least in our neighborhood.

"Why is that, Melanie?" Miss Roach said after a while.

"I don't happen to think there is liberty and justice for all," Melanie said. "What about the South, the Negroes? Where's the justice in lynchings? What kind of liberty is that, with the Ku Klux Klan and starvation wages? They're no better off than slaves. And what about the coal mines? There are vast numbers of people in this country who would gladly swap that

97

so-called liberty and justice for decent work and some self-respect."

It was a long speech and Melanie delivered it with fervor.

"That's a valid point of view," Miss Roach said generously, though she was obviously under a strain. "There are many ills and we must be ever vigilant. But perhaps you are overlooking the spirit of the pledge, the intention, which, after all, is what's important, isn't it, dear? However, if you would prefer to say only that part of the pledge you agree with and be silent during the 'liberty and justice for all' part, I will overlook it."

I thought Miss Roach had handled the crisis nicely, but I was mainly impressed with Melanie's stand. The more I thought about what she'd said, the more I was sorry I hadn't thought of it first. In the next few days it became apparent that she had many ideas and opinions I hadn't thought of. She wasn't aggressive about it, but if called on there wasn't a subject she didn't argue with except geography and spelling. She was a real find.

"Do you want to be friends?" was my opening gambit. It was along about Melanie's fifth day and I had purposely sat next to her in the lunchroom.

"What a lousy sandwich," she said, looking sadly at what she had just bitten into. It was a cucumber sandwich on raisin bread.

"You want half of mine?" I said. "It's tuna fish."

"What's your name?"

"Allegra Maud Goldman."

"Wow," she said. "That's a real potpourri of a name."

"What's a potpourri?" I said.

"What I wish I were having for lunch."

"Why don't you tell your mother you don't like cucumber sandwiches?"

"I make my own sandwiches," she said, giving me an odd, hostile look. "My mother hasn't got time. It's hard for me to think about sandwiches in the morning because I'm never hungry then. I thought this would be a good idea."

"I never heard of cucumber sandwiches."

"The English are always having them for tea," she said, so I knew she was a reader. I forced half my tuna fish sandwich on her and struggled with half her cucumber sandwich and we were friends.

She was the first person I knew who lived in an apartment house. She was also the first product of a broken home I had ever known. Her parents had been divorced for three years and she hardly ever saw her father. I told her I had sometimes tried to talk my mother into divorcing my father but she had never paid any attention.

"What's wrong with your father?" Melanie said.

"He has a terrible temper. He is ill-natured."

It was another week before Melanie invited me to come home after school with her and, although she had refused my invitations, I accepted hers at once. On the way she warned me about her sister, who was called Sister. She was two years younger than Melanie and a pest. Also, as I was bound to discover for myself, she was crazy. Not really crazy, but impossible.

"Is Sister her real name?" I asked.

"No. Her real name is Sophronia. That, laughably, means 'sensible' in Greek."

"Melanie and Sophronia," I said. "Your mother must be very romantic."

"My father named us."

"Why did they get divorced?"

"They fought all the time," Melanie said. "My father is a

highly educated and sensitive man, but he can't seem to earn a living. He's always failing at things. And my mother, who wasn't even born in this country, is a hardheaded business woman. She has a dry-cleaning store.''

She was the first friend I had whose mother worked. There was no end to her firsts. By the time we got to her apartment house I even found *it* glamorous. It was a six-story gray stone building, and the lobby had a marble floor, yellow stucco walls and big, dark Spanish furniture with red velvet upholstery.

"This is gorgeous," I said while we waited for the elevator.

"Gorgeous!" she said. "It's awful."

"Why? It's almost as grand as the Loew's Kings."

"It's tacky," she snapped. "You don't have to be polite."

As we rode slowly up to the fourth floor I wondered why what looked gorgeous to me looked tacky to Melanie, never doubting that Melanie's view was the correct one, since she was so emphatic about it.

"That must be what they mean by 'a question of taste,' " I said. "I guess we have different tastes."

Melanie was getting more and more sullen as the elevator rose.

"Maybe you just don't have *any* taste," she said severely. She was probably right, so I vowed, as the elevator bumped to a halt and the door slid open, to begin to try to have taste. It would mean really looking at things and penetrating what was, to me, a total mystery. I knew from my father's business that what was fashionable and considered to be in good taste one year was no longer fashionable the next; that if you wore last year's style this year people might even laugh at you. It seemed to be true of furniture, too. Even colors could go out of style. And combinations of colors. In those days you wouldn't dream of combining anything blue with green, or black with brown. It was considered revolting.

Melanie opened her apartment door with a key and I followed her inside. It was going to be a lot of trouble having taste, but I began right away by carefully examining everything in the living room, assuming that since it was Melanie's home and she was so knowledgeable, everything in it must be right. There was a scarred old upright piano with some of the ivories missing; a small sofa with jade green upholstery; a pot-bellied commode, also painted jade green, with red-and-gold dragons and blue peacocks and red-and-gold pagodas painted on it; on top of this was the Brooklyn telephone directory; on top of that was the telephone and next to all this was a white china lamp with rosebuds painted on it and a fluted green shade. There were also two overstuffed chairs with round arms, one gold, one another shade of green and a Philco console radio. It was a small room and all of the furniture touched. There was one picture of a windmill and a Dutch boy on the wall.

I was trying to decide how I felt about the room and what comment I should make, or if it would be wiser not to say anything, when Melanie said, "My mother has rotten taste, too. I can't wait to get out of here and have my own place."

It was then that I noticed the ashtray with the pipe in it, and, while Melanie was putting our coats in the closet, I saw a man's overcoat hanging there and a gray fedora on the shelf.

"Are those still your father's things?" I said.

"No, they're Alfred's," Melanie said in an unnaturally nonchalant voice. "He's my mother's paramour."

I began to say "What's a paramour" when my instincts intervened. I could always look it up when I got home. I followed Melanie into the kitchen, a tiny room with a lot happening in it.

"That pest didn't do the dishes," Melanie said in a rage, looking into the sink.

"Your mother?" I asked, shocked.

"Sister. It's her turn today. She never does what she's supposed to do and I always get the blame." She filled a kettle with water and put it on the stove. "We'll have tea," she said.

Tea was something I had only when I was sick and therefore I didn't much care for it, but in that moment it became absolutely the most delightfully correct thing to have.

"That will be lovely," I said, sitting down at the kitchen table, which Melanie was clearing of the remnants of their breakfast. The front door banged and someone called, "Mell? You home?"

"You didn't do the dishes, you turd," Melanie shouted.

Sister appeared in the doorway. She was taller than Melanie and generally constructed on a sturdier, larger scale, and she had round red cheeks and smallish green eyes. She was still carrying her briefcase, an incredibly sloppy one with gashes in it and Band-Aids around the handles and pieces of ink-smudged notepaper sticking out of the top.

"It's your turn today," she said. "Who's that?"

"It's not my turn, you slob, I did them yesterday, and if you don't do them right away I'll kill you, and this time I mean it, you crud."

Sister put down her briefcase and took her hat and coat and muffler off, dropping everything in a heap on the kitchen floor. She came over to the table and sat down opposite me.

"How do you do?" she said sweetly. "I'm Sister, Melanie's sister. Who are you?"

"Allegra Maud Goldman," I said.

"You a friend of *hers?*" she asked unnecessarily, as why else would I have been there. "You're too good for her."

"Melanie is my *best* friend," I said.

"That doesn't say much for your other friends."

"I mean it, Sister, if you don't do the dishes this minute I'll push you out of the window into the airshaft and they'll never be able to get your body out and it will lie there forever stinking with the rest of the garbage down there."

"If you lay a hand on me I'll call Mom. I think I'll call her anyway."

"Don't you dare call her, you horse's ass, don't you dare bother her. She has enough to worry about in that lousy store with customers yelling at her all day without your dumb telephone calls."

The kettle began to scream, too. Melanie turned the gas off under it and brought two cups and saucers and teabags to the table. She put one set in front of me and the other as far from Sister as she could.

"Where's mine?" Sister said.

"You can get it yourself. I'm not your servant." Then, in an entirely different voice, Melanie said to me, "Lemon or cream, Allegra?"

"I always have it with lemon," I said.

"Well, try it with cream. It's much better that way."

"Okay," I said. "Do the customers really yell at your mother?"

"It's disgusting," Melanie said. "They bring in this absolute *dreck* and then they threaten to sue because there's a button off, or they say it shrank, or the color ran, or there's a hole somewhere, and how can you prove that's the way it was when they brought it in? My mother's a wreck by the time she gets home at night."

"She used to have a millinery store," Sister said. "That was much better. But it failed."

"It was a poor location," Melanie explained, putting a box of Nabisco Wafers down in front of me. "Have one."

"Thank you," I said, and took one.

"Me too," Sister said, reaching for the box and grabbing a fistful. "I'm starved. I lost my lunch again."

"Liar. I bet you didn't even go to school. She never goes to school. My mother's always having to see the principal."

"It was raining today," Sister said. "I had to go to school."

"Last year when we were still living in Borough Park she was suspended twice."

"You don't have to tell her everything," Sister said. She reached for her briefcase and rummaged around in it, coming out with a fountain pen and a dog's leash. She carefully fastened the end of the leash to the penclip, then got up and put her hat and coat and muffler back on.

"I have to take my fountain pen out for a walk," she said to me. "You want to come along?"

"No thanks," I said. She left, holding one end of the leash, the pen trailing along the floor at the other. We heard the front door slam.

"Is she really taking her fountain pen for a walk?" I asked.

"Yes. And when she comes to a tree she stops and lets some ink out of the pen."

"What does she do that for?"

"She thinks it's funny. She's disgusting. We had dinner at Garfield's Cafeteria the other night and she had a long conversation with a coat tree. Then she said, 'Oh, I beg your pardon, I thought you were my Uncle Herbert.' She'll do anything for attention. We haven't even got an Uncle Herbert."

Melanie sipped some tea and then she burst into tears.

"And you'll notice," she sobbed, "that she didn't do the dishes."

"Calm down," I said. "Don't cry."

"I wish she were dead."

"No you don't," I said. "She's only a child."

"What would you know? I wish she were dead with all my heart. I even have to sleep in the same bed with her."

The telephone rang and Melanie stopped crying and blew her nose and answered it.

"Hello, Mom," she said. "Yes, fine. Yeah she came home but she's gone out for a walk. How do I know if she actually went, she said she did. Yes, I have the list, I'll take care of it. He didn't? But I have a friend . . . Oh damn, all right. In about twenty minutes." She hung up and turned to me with a look of despair. "The delivery boy didn't show up. I have to go make six deliveries for her."

"Do you want me to go with you?"

"Christ no," she said and burst into tears again. After a while she said, "I'm sorry. I'm at my worst with my family."

"We all are," I said.

That night before dinner, after I had looked up paramour and then had to look up illicit, I went into the living room, where my mother was reading *The New York Sun.* She looked snug and comfortable sitting there in our deepest armchair with her shoes off and her feet up on the ottoman. I could smell the roast beef and apple pie Olga had cooking in the oven.

"Which did you play today, bridge or mah-jongg?" I asked.

"Neither," my mother said, not looking up. "I went to a luncheon at the Waldorf for the Kadesh Barnea Society for the Helpless Hebrew Aged, and then I went to McCreery's."

"What did they have for lunch?"

"What they always have," my mother said. "Broiled

chicken with grapes and cocoanut ice cream balls. And they had a fashion show."

"What did you buy at McCreery's?"

My mother looked up from the paper. "You're full of questions today. There was a linen sale so I bought some sheets and pillow cases. And I bought myself a couple of girdles."

"You're a lucky woman," I said.

"You think so? Wait till your father gets the bill."

"We all have our problems," I said.

Chapter 9

The Place was what we always called my father's place of business, which occupied the entire twelfth floor of a skyscraper on Seventh Avenue and Fortieth Street. I hated going there but sometimes it was unavoidable. Now that I was getting so tall it was even more unavoidable than usual, as my father had decided that I could begin wearing his garments instead of imposing on his friend Irving Walkowitz, who made Dolly Dimple Preteen Frocks. I had hated going there, too, but my mother insisted that I had to try things on to make sure they were becoming. Becoming what, I always asked. My father's garments were certainly not becoming. They were designed for wealthy matrons, cost a lot of money and came in sizes all the way up to obese. No matter how carefully these dresses were fitted to me, I always felt like a freak in them because they were designed to have bosoms in the tops and hips in the bottoms, items I was unable to supply.

The chief reason I hated going there, though, was that it was the one place where I entirely lost any connection with the person I thought I was and became someone totally different: the boss's daughter, a complete stranger to me, an identity I bumbled around in feeling inadequate, graceless, tongue-tied and false. How I envied David, whose knickers came to him in a cardboard box. It was one dumb conversation after another with people who treated me as though I were her royal highness, a princess with a pea-sized brain.

GOLD-MODES, MAX GOLDMAN, INC. were the first words to greet you when you stepped off the elevator, though there had already been a conversation with Joe, the elevator starter. Directly above these words behind a sliding-glass partition, wedged between switchboard and typewriter, was the carefully coiffed head of Millie Brodsky, receptionist, deliverer of the next words: "Well, will you look who's here. How nice to see your fresh young face, dearie."

"Glunk," I said, trying to decide whether to enter left to the showroom or right to the shipping room. I opted for left in the hope of fewer conversations. The showroom was a big, plush, blue and gray room with partitioned cubicles where buyers could sit behind little glass-topped tables writing orders while models waltzed before them parading the current line and salesmen hovered, buttering them up and touting the wares. No customers today. Just Mr. Feldman and Mr. Cohen, two of the salesmen, swapping the usual dirty stories.

"Good day, Madam," Feldman said, rearranging his crotch. "What can I sell you today?"

"Glunk," I said, not breaking my stride. Through a draped opening into the models' brightly lit cave, all mirrors at one end, racks down the other, on which hung the demonstration goods. Three models, Marlene, Charlotte and Laverne, were sitting in their underwear smoking cigarettes and drinking coffee out of soggy containers, watching themselves in the mirror through glazed eyes.

"Glunk," they said to me. "Glunk," I replied.

Into the office, a dreary place full of arithmetic, bookkeepers making entries in ledgers, making out payrolls, making deposits, and secretaries typing letters saying, "Re: your order #359685 we regret that we are unable to supply our model #0058B, size 18, of which you ordered three (3) in champagne and are therefore substituting the sauterne, a popular shade. Please let us know if this is acceptable or if you would prefer the liebfraumilch."

Off this beehive was, my father's office, a narrow, windowless, no-nonsense chamber with a big leather sofa and an even bigger desk, a coat tree sprouting his hat, overcoat, suit jacket, and umbrella, his rubbers neatly toed-in at the roots. I peered in. My father was going over some sketches of the upcoming line with the designer, Gus Quinzanero. Both men were in their shirtsleeves, but there the similarity ended. My father's shirts were always white, often white on white (a man who couldn't get enough white in his shirts, a conservative dresser), the knot of his tie loosened. Gus Quinzanero's shirt was blush-hued, his impeccable flannel trousers held high by broad scarlet suspenders with pictures of the king, queen and jack running up and down them.

"Crap," my father was saying. "The same warmed-over crap. Cancel that one."

"You're a real bitch today, Max," the designer said amiably. "But so what else is new?" He was the only one of my father's 150 employees allowed to talk to him that way. My mother said this was because he could go almost anywhere tomorrow and get as good a job or better, and what's worse, could go into business for himself and compete with my father.

My father looked up as I slid quietly into a corner of the sofa. His face rarely lighted up at the sight of me; if it changed at all it was to sour even further.

"I'm busy now," he said. "Can't you see I'm busy?"

I went into the factory, first to the cutting room, where the cutters, important men, were slicing around patterns through layers of costly fabrics. One false move and *disaster.* There was another huge room where the operators sat going blind over their whirring-machines, and several smaller rooms for patternmakers, drapers and pressers. The factory people were mainly foreign-born, Italian and Jewish, and it was they who treated me with such subservience and respect that if I were not too busy gagging I would have leapt onto a table and cried (with a nod to Melanie), "Workers of the world unite. Break the chains that bind you!" Though according to my father they were already solidly united, and between the crooked unions and the gangster truckers and the sonofabitch landlords, he was being squeezed like a blackhead out of his own business that he built with the honest manly sweat of his brow in order to give employment and livelihood to all these people who would otherwise be starving and lying around in gutters with festering sores on their eyes, to say nothing of leprosy and cholera.

"Your father makes his wealth off the backs of the honest poor," said Melanie when she learned he was a Capitalist, an employer. "Every mouthful you eat is carved from the flesh of some simple, honest, upright, noble, exploited workingman coughing his lungs out in an unsanitary shop. For shame."

Though to be perfectly honest it was not an unsanitary place, and the only people I ever actually saw sweating there were my father and the pressers, and pressers would sweat anywhere, as would my father.

I was waiting for my mother, who was going to select my wardrobe for the coming season. She would go through the size tens in the stockroom and select those she thought were becoming, and then Sophie, the seamstress, would appear with pins in her mouth and her hands full of chalk and rulers and together they would decide on the necessary adjustments. Meanwhile, I had nothing to do. I foraged around, looking for treasures to swipe. I collected scraps of material from the cutting room floor and stuffed them into a bag. These I would take home and, in a month or two, throw away, as I could never think of anything to do with them. While I was browsing among the cuttings I heard my father, finished now with Gus, screaming at Agnes Mortadella. Agnes's bailiwick was a cage at one end of the cutting room. Inside the cage were shelves filled with boxes of buttons and belt buckles. This was the trimming department, and Agnes, a short, stocky woman with a nervous mouth and intense eyes, was in charge of all the trimmings, a responsible position. My father was yelling at her now about some buttons.

"They break, fa chrissake. They break right in their fingers. How the hell do you expect them to sew them on, fa chrissake, they're made of matzoth."

"I'm sorry, Mr. Goldman, I'll take care of it."

"Who the hell sold you these lousy buttons?"

"I'll look it up, Mr. Goldman."

"Don't you know? You're supposed to know these things. What the hell do you think I'm paying you for?"

"Here it is, Mr. Goldman, it's Superior-Rivkin. I'll call them right now."

"Goddamn sons of bitches, tell them we sew on buttons, fa chrissake, not crackers. Don't you feel the goddamned buttons before you buy them?"

"I can't feel all the buttons, Mr. Goldman, be reasonable."

"Don't stand there and tell me to be reasonable, fa chrissake, I'll throw you right out in the street where you came from."

By this time Agnes Mortadella was crying hard enough to make my father feel better, so he stormed off to some greener pasture. I sidled up to Agnes's cage.

"Oh, hello, Allegra," she said, blowing her nose.

"Why don't you quit?" I said. "How can you let anyone talk to you that way?"

She was on the telephone. "Just a minute," she said to me. "Hello, Superior-Rivkin? Let me talk to Bernie." She put her hand over the mouthpiece, waiting. "Your father can kiss my ass on 42nd street. Hello Bernie, you shit. That lot number WJZ127936. No, not that one. Yeah, those. Oh, you know about it, whadderyou, some kind of jokers up there? You better haul your ass right over here. Not four o'clock, right now, or I'll throw the whole entire order back at you and good-bye Superior-Rivkin where Gold-Modes is concerned." She banged the two halves of the phone back together.

"Now, what were you saying, darling?"

"Why do you stand for it? Why don't you work for someone else? There must be lots of jobs for someone of your caliber."

She gave me a long look while she chewed her underlip.

"They're all the same," she said. "You think any of them are any better? You know how long I'm working for your father? Since the day he went into business. I was only fourteen. I lied. The way I was built I could get away with it."

"I don't understand it," I said. "I *have* to put up with him. I *can't* quit. But you."

"Oh, he's all right, your father," she said. "That's just the way he is. But fair's fair, he's someone you can count on."

"What do you mean?"

"He's as good as his word. He's an honest, dependable man."

She really liked my father. It was beyond all understanding, though I strained.

"You know what he makes me feel?" she said. "Safe. My own old man was much worse. He used to chain me to the bed so I wouldn't go out and screw with boys. After him, your father's a saint."

My mother appeared then, so I took my leave of Agnes and went back to the models' room, where we got down to business. Forewarned, I was wearing a clean, practically new slip, but oh how I hated to stand there in it between selections with all sorts of people, including Cohen and Feldman, walking through. No privacy and everyone a kibbitzer.

"That looks very nice on you," my mother said. "Don't you think that looks nice, Allegra?" I glanced into the mirror and made a face. "Well, do you like it or don't you? You're the one who's going to have to wear it." What was there to like about a dress? Or to choose between one and another? Either it had buttons down the front or it didn't; it had a collar or it hadn't; the collar was pointed or round. There was no choice when it came to sleeves, as all Gold-Mode frocks, except in summer, had bracelet-length sleeves, very flattering to skinny arms and bony wrists.

Sophie, who was kneeling on the floor at my hem, said through the pins in her mouth, "That's *her* color. Look how it makes those eyes look."

"It's a little too long in the front," my mother said.

"I'm fixing. Don't worry, it'll be perfect."

"Stand up straight," my mother said.

My father, passing through, glanced at me with genuine

displeasure and, not pausing, said, *"Shlump."*

"Shoulders back, stomach in. Like this," Marlene said, coming out of her coma and actually getting up off her chair to demonstrate standing.

"Gorgeous," Feldman said on his way to the toilet. "Next year she can come and model for us."

"It isn't right up here," my mother said to Sophie, pointing at my chest where the dress, as always, sagged dispiritedly.

"We'll put darts," Sophie said, sticking in pins. "I'll tell you what you should do, Allegra darling, just in the meantime till they grow in. Wear a brassiere and stuff it with socks.

"Glunk," I said.

"I mean it. You'd be surprised how many women do it."

"Fa chrissake," I said.

"How do you like this nice polka dot, Allegra? It has a nice little bolero jacket. It'll cover up your chest."

"How the hell many dresses are you getting her, fa chrissake?" my father said, passing through now in the opposite direction. "Where the hell is she going in all those dresses, on a cruise?"

"Yeah? Where the hell am I going?" I said.

"All what dresses?" my mother said. "Two, so far."

"You know what that number sells for?" my father said of the polka dot with the little bolero. "Forty-nine ninety-five wholesale. That's a hundred-dollar number in Bonwit's."

"I don't even want it," I said.

"Never mind," my mother said for my father's benefit. "Your cousin Sonia never walks out of here with less than eight dresses at a time. You're certainly entitled to two, the boss's daughter."

"I have a headache."

"You want some aspirin, darling?" Sophie said. "I have

114

some aspirin right by my machine."

"Walk away, Allegra. Let me see how that looks walking."

I did my cripple's walk.

"Allegra! Walk properly."

I did my regular walk. My father, slashing through the room again in time to observe this, said, "Can't she learn to walk like a human being?" Once again Marlene tore her eyes from her reflection and rose to her feet, this time to give lessons in walking.

"Like this, dear heart. Make believe you've got a book on your head. Wait, I'll go find an actual book and you can try it," she said, vanishing gracefully.

"She's at the awkward age," my mother said to anyone present who happened to need that information.

"I've got a splitting headache," I whimpered. Socks on my chest, books on my head, what next?

"Little Cuban heels, that's the ticket," Feldman said on his way back from the toilet. "That number don't look so hot with saddle shoes."

"Where's Cohen?" I said. "We're waiting for his comments."

"Oh, look at this smart little spectator sport, Allegra," said my mother. "It's just the thing."

"Not one single goddamn book in this entire place," Marlene reappeared to say. "Nothing but phone books and ledgers, and they're too heavy."

"Thanks anyway," I said, "but we're finished walking."

"Try this on, Allegra," my mother said. "It's adorable, even though it isn't your size."

"We'll put darts," Sophie said.

"I can't get out of this one," I said. "It's pinned to my slip. Maybe to my flesh. I think I have to throw up."

"Stop that nonsense, Allegra," my mother said while Sophie unpinned me from the little polka dot number. "It's all in your head."

"It is?" I said, and a moment later it was out of my head and all over the cute little bolero.

Chapter 10

My father learned his yelling from his mother, who was excellent at it. It was something she did every chance she got, but during the time I knew her she only had poor Grandpa to yell at, and he had solved that problem by going deaf. He was a short, compact, benign-looking man with thin red hair and a small red moustache beneath which he usually wore a small, oblivious smile no matter how hard Grandma was hollering or what the subject. She was in a perpetual rage at him but he had outwitted her and they both knew it.

His deafness also prevented Grandpa from entering into conversations, but I doubt if he had ever been much of a talker. About the only thing he ever said to me was, "Have some," as whenever he saw David or me he would make a beeline for the dish of raisins and walnuts to pass around.

I often tried to imagine what his life could have been like inside his head but I never had a clue. When he died he didn't leave a trace of himself apart from the few clothes he owned and his dentures and eyeglasses. Except for passing around fruit and nuts, the only thing I ever saw him do was read *The Forward.*

If Grandma Goldman ever smiled, she must have done it in the bathroom with the door locked. She had been the undisputed head of her own family, ruling with an iron hand and a mouth full of rocks. It was she who had run the grocery store, too, as Grandpa tended to give things away to anyone with a hard-luck story, and back then where they lived that was practically everybody. It was she who scrimped and saved and made canny little investments in real estate so that in time they could give up the store and live on a small income. They lived in the upper half of a two-family house in the Crown Heights section of Brooklyn, above a lady dental technician whom Grandma reverently called Doctor. Because they had one bedroom too many, they also had a paying boarder, referred to by Grandma as "montenna." He was a flashy ex-bootlegger named Jack Tarshis, a widower in his sixties who spent most of his time at the track and the rest of it vainly courting the lady dental technician.

Grandma Goldman was in our kitchen now, in a frenzy of baking. The worst of the Depression was over so my mother and father were taking a trip to Mexico. Our distaff Grandma, who would normally have been in charge, as she was already in residence, was paying a visit to her sister Gussie, who had a chicken farm in Washingtonville, New York, so my parents had fingered the Goldman grandparents to stay with us. It was the first and last time this would happen. David and I had protested, since, after all, we had Olga and Arthur and we were no longer babies, but my mother said she would rest easier. Not that she was doing any resting in Mexico, judging from the postcards that came almost daily from one unpronounceable place after another.

It was Friday and Grandma was baking challah and onion rolls. When she had all the goods out of the oven and cooling there wasn't an empty surface in the kitchen. It was a whole-sale operation.

"Who's going to eat all that?" I said.

"It's for the whole week. I only bake once a week."

I counted. There were eighteen long loaves and sixty-five rolls. Grandma's baking hand was as heavy as her personality, so even fresh from the oven you could barely lift one of her breads unless you had taken a mail-order course that trans-formed you from a ninety-five pound weakling. By Sunday, if you dropped one of her onion rolls on your foot, you'd have broken every toe. By Tuesday, when you threw out what was left over (because what else could you do with it?), you could hear the garbage man groaning. But Grandma didn't throw out so fast. When she finally acknowledged the extent of the overkill, she tried to palm it off by calling everyone she could think of (all relatives) to come and get a loaf. Nobody came. This did not prevent her from repeating the identical exercise the following week.

It was a real drag for David and me. The minute David sat down at the piano, Grandpa would come into the living room to read his newspaper. He could barely hear the piano but what he heard he enjoyed. However, Grandma would be right at his heels, hollering at him about something, like why was he wearing those socks, she didn't have a chance yet to fix the hole, it would only get bigger. And if I sat down to read, it was Grandma's cue to sit nearby and have a conversa-tion with me, as it was obvious to her that I wasn't doing anything. Grandma couldn't read and I don't think she had any notion what reading was. I believe she thought it was merely an excuse for lowering your eyes.

Grandma's idea of conversation was to ask questions she already knew the answers to, such as, "You're wearing your new blue dress today?" or "Papa and Mama are still in Mexico?" Or else she would tell you something she knew you already knew. All her statements began with, "If God is good to me," and went on to outline what she was going to do ten or fifteen minutes hence if out of God's goodness she was granted that much longer to live. She trusted God about as much as she'd have trusted a left-handed gambler with a diamond tooth.

She was an inveterate hypochondriac, and about four times a week she went to one doctor or another just to check up on God. She also had doctors she went to to check up on the other doctors. They all got tired of seeing her and told her to go home and take Carter's Little Liver Pills.

Fortunately, the cigar store on Avenue J had just begun to feature practical joke items. David was studying with a Hebrew teacher after school, as his bar mitzvah was not far off, and he had to pass the cigar store on his way home. Between the dreariness of the Hebrew lessons and the bleakness of what lay ahead at home, it was inevitable that David would be attracted by the cigar store's new window display and he became their best customer.

We planned a restrained campaign, only one a day, just for leavening. Grandma fell for everything: the puddle of ink on the carpet that she carefully, after a piercing scream, scooped up with a tablespoon; the poo-poo cushion she sat down on and leaped right up from; the wobbling plate she kept trying to steady with one hand while eating chicken noodle soup with the other; the dribble glass and the butterflies that flew out from under the platter of gefillte fish when she picked it up to pass to Grandpa. Each time the joke was revealed, Grandpa would laugh so hard he would have a coughing fit and tears would stream down his cheeks, while Grandma muttered angrily that she hadn't been fooled, she "knew it all the time."

The enormous joy Grandpa took in the tricks we played on Grandma did our hearts good; it was the only time we had ever seen him come to life. We could tell that as the day wore on Grandpa was looking forward eagerly to that evening's entertainment, becoming more alert and watchful, his eyes fairly twinkling with anticipation. After the first week, we ran out of store-bought gadgets and, not wanting to let Grandpa down, had to resort to invention. Because Grandma was a lintpicker, we tucked a spool of white thread in the breast pocket of David's jacket and threaded one end through his lapel, where it curled innocently until Grandma spotted it and reached to pluck it off. Grandma's challah came to the dinner table hacked into thick slices and stacked on the bread tray. As soon as we noticed that Grandma never asked anyone please to pass the bread, but struck out with a fork, stabbing the top slab, we naturally figured out a way to string all the slices together.

By the time our parents came home from Mexico, Grandma was more than ready to leave, but poor Grandpa dragged his heels, looking wistfully over his shoulder.

"Why don't we keep Grandpa?" I said to my mother. "Grandma doesn't need him for anything."

"Don't be silly," my mother said. "They're husband and wife."

Soon afterwards, it was time for David's bar mitzvah, and there he stood, graduated from knickers into his first real suit with long pants, a yarmulke perched on his head, the tallith across his shoulders, at last at the forefront of the stage, thanking our mother and father for having guided him so accurately through the perilous shoals of childhood to the shores of manhood where, now firmly planted on his own two feet, he vowed to do them, his ancestors and all of Jewry, as well as the world at large, honor by endeavoring to keep his shoulder to the wheel, his nose to the grindstone, his ear to the ground, his eye on the sparrow, his hands clean, his heart pure and his lips sealed against profanity, sacrilege and sedition. It was a tall order, but the torch had been passed along to him and he would do all in his power to keep its flame steady and bright until such time as it was given him to pass it on. He was proud to be the son of his parents and he hoped to make them, in turn, proud to be the parents of himself.

Since his voice had not yet changed and had in fact begun with a quaver of nervousness before settling into a barely audible and much-too-rapid monotone, and since he stood not much higher than he had at the age of ten, I looked around to see if anyone was convinced. It was hard to tell about my father and Grandpa Goldman, as they were sitting downstairs among the men, the fathers, uncles and brothers of that day's five bar mitvah youths, a mass of dark suits and hunched shoulders and yarmulkes and prayer shawls. The females were not allowed to sit in the orchestra so I was upstairs, a pariah among my own kind. I looked at my mother and grandmothers and they appeared to be moved, but it was by the occasion rather than by their segregation. It was my first time in a *shule* and I had not been forewarned about the sexual arrangement.

"What are they afraid of?" I had asked my mother. "That we'll take their minds off higher things if we mingle with them in God's house?"

"Shhh! It's the tradition. You can look up why when you get home."

"This is the hayloft," I muttered.

"Be quiet. Who do you think you are to question thousands of years of religious tradition?"

Who *did* I think I was? Who was I? Allegra Maud Goldman wearing a new powder blue spring coat. I sank deeper into my leper's chair, thankful only for Grandpa. Here, at least, in the temple of the lord, he had the edge on Grandma, he was a man among men. He was the only example I could think of to justify the disgraceful seating arrangement.

But it was David's day and God bless him. I sat without fidgeting through all the preliminaries, and I even prayed a little that David wouldn't die of nervousness, as I knew how he had been dreading this day for months and months. I had even offered to write his English speech for him because I had a few ideas about what should be in it, but he had declined. Needless to say, the speech he gave contained none of my ideas.

When the ceremony was over, we ladies were permitted to descend to an antechamber where everyone gathered, somewhat as equals, to eat little coffee cakes and drink schnapps. Probably from relief, everyone was extraordinarily jolly. My father had his arm around David's shoulder. His face was flushed and he was grinning broadly, asking everyone what they thought of his young man and wasn't David's the best goddamned speech of the day.

"You made it all up yourself, David?" he said. "I really liked it, that about the sea and the shoals and the shore and all that. Very poetic. Who knows, maybe he'll turn out to be a lawyer. What do you think, David?"

David shrugged. Naturally, he had no intention of being a lawyer.

"Because to be a piano player you don't need such a silver

tongue, right, David? Have some cake."

My father downed his third shot of schnapps neat, and didn't, I noticed, offer any to David, in spite of David's having that very moment achieved manhood.

"The perilous shoals of childhood," my father mused. "That's pretty good. But what was so perilous about *your* childhood?"

"Well, you know, chicken pox and measles and all that," David mumbled.

I sidled over to the festive board and rapidly downed a Scotch, hoping to quell my disgust, and while I was choking and gagging, my mother, from whom it was impossible to conceal anything, told me that it served me right and that I would receive further punishment at a later date.

We dispersed, to regather later that day at our house for the big party. We lived only a few blocks from the synagogue, so my parents, David, Grandma and I walked home. My mother held onto my arm, fearful that I might fall down drunk, or at the least, need steering, though I felt perfectly normal. My father walked with David and for a while, because Ocean Avenue has a wide sidewalk, we were able to walk five abreast. The midmorning boozing had gotten to my father. His color was high and he kept a hand on David's shoulder while, all the way home, he uncharacteristically indulged in an incessant, cheery monologue. I'm sure he thought he and David were having a conversation.

"This is a proud day in a man's life," he said. "I don't know how it is with other men, Catholics or *schvartzers,* but for a Jew it's a big thrill, first *having* a son, then the circumcision and then the big day, today. I can remember my own bar mitzvah, though by that time I was a lot further along than you. I had been bringing money into the house for years by then, but I realize it's different for you, you've had more advantages thanks to me, and your mother doesn't understand that you have to be tough to be a man . . ."

My mother said, "You can take a nap when we get home, Max."

". . . I mean it's not as though you're really a man just because you're thirteen years old, and God knows I wish I understood you better, but even so I'm glad I have a son to carry on the name and maybe, I mean it's always a man's hope, the business, too. I mean maybe when you're a little older you'll take some interest, after all, what am I working so hard to build it up for, strangers? Not that it looks much like it now, with all that piano playing. But don't get me wrong, I'm proud of the way you've stuck to it and how good you are at it. Don't I always try to make you play for company? What do you think that is if not that I'm proud of you? But I wish you weren't so timid about it. After all, if you're going to be a concert pianist, God forbid, you have to be more aggressive.

"I know I don't always show my feelings so well, but that doesn't mean I don't have them. It's just that if we had feelings in our day we didn't go around talking about them. We just had them. Nowadays people talk about their feelings *too* much, if you ask me."

"Grandma Goldman is always talking about how rotten she feels," I said.

"Not that kind of feelings. That's health. She always has something to say, that sister of yours."

"Girls," David said.

"But you know what I'm talking about, don't you, David? What I'm trying to say is we were too busy to pay so much attention to our feelings in those days, but that doesn't mean I didn't like music. Didn't I work a whole year after school delivering delicatessen to save up for a violin? Half the money always had to go to my mother, but I saved every penny of my half for that violin and then I had to work for my lessons, too. A quarter a week. I just wonder if you had to work to save up to buy your own piano what you would be playing. A harmonica, probably."

"Buy my own piano?" David said stupidly.

"Sure, that's unheard of, isn't it? A piano comes with the house like the bathroom and the garage, right? You never stopped to think of that, did you?"

"Stop getting yourself excited, Max," my mother said.

"Who's excited? I'm just pointing out. That's one of the advantages I'm always talking about that you kids have that I never had. And did my mother ever even encourage me? She made fun of the violin. She thought it was a foolish waste of time."

"Is that why you quit playing?" I asked.

"I quit playing because I was too busy with other things, making a living. But I was pretty good at it, the fiddle. I bet I could still play some of those pieces. *Liebestraum.* Where is that fiddle, is it still in the attic?"

"Sure," David said. "I'll get it down when we get home."

And that was the first thing David did, even though the caterers had arrived and were beginning to transform our home into a bar and grill. The first thing I did was take my new hat out to the back yard and burn it, as I planned to get through the remainder of my life without ever again wearing a hat. When I got back to the living room, my father was tightening the bow strings and then David gave him an A and he began to tune the fiddle. There was an odd, bemused look on his face while he did this, and it grew even more odd and bemused when, satisfied that the fiddle was properly prepared, he tucked it under his chin, arranged the fingers of his left hand and raised the bow. I looked at David seated at the piano, and saw mirrored on his face what I was feeling: fear of the worst. Then, with great assurance, our father swept the bow across the strings and the violin sang, surprisingly sweet and pure. With his eyes closed and his lips curled in a loving half-smile, he played about ten bars of *Liebestraum* before faltering. I held my breath the whole time, almost awed. There really *was* music in my father. And, as unlike him as David was, this was something, an inadvertent gift, that had passed from my father to his son. It was so mysterious, so unexpected, so beautiful, that my eyes filled with tears. I couldn't help wondering what else lay buried, dammed up forever by the circumstances of his life, in my father's genes, cells, chromosomes—wherever it is that talent, and maybe even genius, reside, whimpering for a while before they suffocate and die.

My father fumbled, trying for the next, forgotten notes, then gave up.

"Not bad after twenty-five years, eh?" he said, gently laying the violin away in its case. "I bet you didn't know your old man could to that."

"Why don't we get some music?" David said, trying to keep the eagerness out of his voice. "We could play together."

Something hung in the air, then, and again I held my breath, waiting. Later, when I had time to think about it, I would begin to understand the faint hope, the desperate plea in David's casual proposal. *We could play together.*

My father shrugged. "Maybe some day," he said, "if I ever have the time." Then, yawning, he went upstairs to take a nap.

A few weeks later, Grandpa Goldman caught pneumonia and swiftly and quietly died.

His was the first death in our family during my lifetime,

except for a great-grandmother on my father's side who died when I was five. I had seen her only a few times, when we visited her in some dim basement apartment, staying only long enough for my father to exchange a few Yiddish words with her and to stuff some money into the white lace pocket of her long, dusty black dress. She was in her nineties and she smelled musty and poor and seemed so ancient to me that I was frightened of her, as though she were not quite human. But when I heard that she had died I made myself cry by imagining her floating in the huge night in that long black dress and by telling myself that she had once been a child, and that she was my ancestor, and that some of her blood, and who knew what else, was mixed with mine.

But with Grandpa it was different. When he died, nobody was prepared for it. David and I went to the funeral and I made myself look at him in the coffin, though I was trembling because I had no idea what to expect. He looked all right, a little paler but not much different than he had always looked except for the times he had laughed at our tricks. When they put the lid on the coffin, my father took out a handkerchief and I could see he was really sobbing. That made me cry, too, as I had never seen my father cry. We went to the cemetery, and when they lowered the coffin into the grave, Grandma began to scream and holler that she was going to throw herself "into the ground," too. It took only one person to restrain her.

Though the shiva-sitting was at our house, my mother made us go to school the next day. I was having breakfast when the front doorbell rang, so I went to answer it. Without a word, nine almost identical small men with long beards and umbrellas filed in, put their umbrellas in the umbrella stand, and bent down to remove their rubbers. It wasn't even raining. I flew upstairs and woke my mother.

"There's a whole band of funny little men with beards downstairs," I screamed. "They just barged right in."

"They've come to say Kaddish for Grandpa," my mother said, closing her eyes. "The prayer for the dead. They'll be coming all week."

My father, who had been showering, came into the bedroom in his underwear.

"They're here?" he said, rummaging in his closet for a suit appropriate to the occasion. All the suits in his closet were appropriate.

"I never knew Grandpa had so many friends," I said, glad to discover this about him. "In fact, I didn't know he had any."

"They're not his friends," my mother said.

"The temple sent them for the minyan. You can't say Kaddish without a minyan," my father said.

"What's a minyan?"

"Ten."

"And they didn't even know Grandpa?"

"They're total strangers."

I sat down on the edge of the bed and tried to digest this information while my father buttoned his shirt.

"What's Kaddish?" I said. "What do you tell God in that kind of prayer?"

"You praise God," my father said. "I guess it's a way of asking God to accept Grandpa in heaven."

"Why would total strangers who didn't know him do that?"

"They're paid to do it," my father said. "They're very religious men and that's one of their duties."

"Why couldn't *we* all do it?" I said. "We *knew* him."

"It has to be all men," my father said.

"You mean to tell me God wouldn't listen if it was women praying? God would rather listen to a bunch of strangers than to his wife and family and friends if some of them happened to be women?"

"That's the way it's done," my father said. "That's the tradition."

"You'll be late for school," my mother said.

All that week the bearded strangers came twice every day with their hats and prayer shawls and my father joined them down in the basement where they stood around the Ping-Pong table swaying and chanting to God on Grandpa's behalf. Fewer of them came in the evening because by that time my uncles were there to help out.

"The men have this religion all sewed up," I said to David. "There must be some religion that thinks girls are people, too."

"Why would they think that?" David said.

Grandma, who stayed with us all that week, did a lot of moaning and sighing. I had never seen her show the least sign of affection for Grandpa while he was alive and could have appreciated it. She had never even called him by his first name. "Goldman," is what she always called him, the first consonant rasping as though it were being run over sandpaper. She hadn't even been kind to him. Put upon was what she always was, and aggravation was all she ever admitted to having received from him. Yet here she was genuinely mourning him, the love of her life. Fifty-two years together. I began, then, to suspect that what people called love might not have anything at all to do with love, and that they could go through life without even knowing it.

Toward the end of that week, Grandma caught a little cold and lost her voice. As she no longer had anything much to do with it, and no one to yell at, she never regained it. For the rest of her life she could talk only in a harsh stage whisper. I knew then that Grandpa had gotten into heaven and God had given him one wish.

Chapter 11

That summer at camp the girls in my age group were having crushes. That's what they called them: crushes. They never said the word love. I spent a lot of time in my favorite beech tree trying to figure out what was a crush and what was love. I will return to that.

Each girl had chosen a counselor on whom to have her crush. If you decided to have a crush, you had to choose a counselor who was not already taken. I made up my mind that if everyone else was going to have a crush, I had better have one, too. I made a list of all the counselors who were not yet taken and although I liked some of them well enough, there wasn't one on whom I wanted to have a crush. So then I asked myself which one I'd choose if I had complete freedom of choice and the answer was Hank, as I already admired everything about her: her smile, her looks, the way she moved, not only the way she played the violin, but the dreamy inward look on her face when she was playing it, the way she had with horses and the grace with which she rode them. Everything about her seemed worthy of emulation. Perhaps because she was a musician, even her voice was lovely, and she never used it to say anything vulgar, pointless or silly. Although she had a sense of humor, she was a serious person with a great deal of reserve and dignity. The more I thought about her the more I had a crush on her. It was as though all I had to do in order to have a crush was to decide to have it. And at that point it was out of my hands.

There were two rainy weeks when, most of our regular activities curtailed, we sat around and talked. Bull sessions, we called them, although as far as I could see they were ordinary conversations.

"Do you realize that Legg is the only one here who hasn't got a crush on anyone?" Naomi Albrecht said one day when six of us were sitting around in a corner of the social hall. Legg had become my nickname that summer, thanks to an uncommon spurt of growth, most of it in that region.

"Maybe she isn't normal," Estelle Moscowitz kindly offered.

"There *is* someone," I said. "I just don't talk about it. I happen to think some things are private."

"You're making it up," Mitzi Swerdlow taunted.

"No, I'm not."

"Who is it, then?"

"Well, all right," I said. "It's Hank."

"*Hank!*" Mitzi shrieked. "But she's *my* crush."

"I can't help that. She's the one I love."

"*Love?*" they all screamed. They were as shocked as though I'd said something obscene.

"Yes," I said. "She's the one I'm in love with."

"*In love with!*" they chorused, outraged. "You can't be in

love with her. She's a woman. She's the same sex."

"All right, then," I sighed. "She's the one I've got a crush on."

"Well you can't," Mitzi said. "She's *my* crush."

"For heaven's sake," I said, "I'm not planning to marry her or anything." In fact, I had no idea what you were supposed to do with a crush once you had it. "I can't help my feelings."

"It isn't fair," Naomi said.

"Why don't you have a crush on Judson?" Jennifer Berg suggested. "Nobody's using her."

"I don't happen to feel that way about Judson. Listen, who made up the rules? Where is it written?"

They thought about that for ten seconds and then Naomi, who was a few months older than the rest of us and had, therefore, in matters of the heart, assumed a certain leadership, said, "That's just the way it is. That's the way it's always been."

"Not as far as I'm concerned," I said firmly.

They looked at me with what I thought was a certain amount of respect, so I went on. "You can't legislate your feelings." Where had I read that? "If you like someone you like them, and the devil take the hindmost."

"Well, I'm going to tell Hank that I had a crush on her first," Mitzi said in an aggrieved voice. "And not to pay any attention to yours."

"Tell her whatever you like," I said. "Do you *really* tell them you have a crush on them?"

"How else would they know?"

"What do they say?"

"They act embarrassed, or they say don't be silly, or something like that."

"I pick blueberries for Aitch and leave them at her place at dinner every night," Naomi said.

"I make funny valentines for Casey," Estelle said. "I mail them to her with actual stamps."

"What do you do, Jennifer?" I said.

"I just sort of follow Horsey around," she said. "I go swimming whenever I can." Horsey was the swimming instructor. "I haven't been able to think of anything else to do. But I'm getting to be a marvelous swimmer."

"What do you plan to do about Hank?" Mitzi asked acidly.

"I don't plan to do anything," I said. "I didn't know you were supposed to."

"Oh, well, then, that's all right."

I escaped to my beech tree as soon after that as I could, though the leaves were still damp from the rain. My beech tree had a crotched bough that was as comfortable to lie in as a hammock. Although it was right outside the social hall and had a bench circling its trunk, no one had ever yet looked up and spied me in it, so it was still a secret place. I have never been able to figure out why people so rarely do look up. Although I had no intention of eavesdropping, people sat beneath me under that tree many a time and had long and possibly private conversations without ever once suspecting that there might be someone right above them in that tree.

It was midway through my first summer at Camp Stowe and I had long since stopped hating it. I hadn't wanted to go, and when the subject first came up I resisted fiercely. They had tried both David and me out at camp the summer I was eight and it hadn't worked. I had lasted out that summer, miserable and homesick, but David, after less than two weeks, managed to get stricken with acute appendicitis. My father had to charter a private plane and he and Dr. Wise flew to New Hampshire to get David. When they got back to Floyd Bennett

Airport an ambulance was waiting to rush David to the hospital for his operation, and there was a story about it in *The Brooklyn Daily Eagle* headed: LOCAL DRESS MAN FLIES STRICKEN SON FROM N.H. CAMP. Imagine something like that making the newspapers today.

"I don't see why I have to go," I protested. "David doesn't, and he's already had his appendix out."

"David is too sensitive to go to camp," my mother said.

"I'm sensitive, too," I said. "I just try not to show it."

"I made a mistake when I sent you to Camp Caribou. You were too young. You'll like this camp."

"I'll hate it," I said.

My father was always pointing out how expensive Camp Stowe was and telling my mother that there were plenty of perfectly good camps that cost half as much, but for once my mother was adamant. So now my mother was the one to remind me that Camp Stowe was expensive and that I should therefore be grateful. I couldn't see what possible difference the cost could make, but it turned out she was right.

For one thing, it was a beautiful camp in the Massachusetts Berkshires. I hadn't been there long before I fell in love with the countryside—the woods, the lake, the gentle green mountains, the special blue of the sky, the sunlight and sunsets and the rolling meadows dotted with wildflowers.

Then, too, because Camp Stowe could afford to pay its counselors decent salaries, they weren't just kids looking for a free summer, but older women in their twenties, many of whom taught in New England women's colleges and specialized in something like painting or dramatics. My counsellor, whose name was Henrietta but whom everyone called Hank, was a professional violinist, one of the camp's chamber group. The group gave candlelight recitals two evenings a week. We weren't required to go, and if we did we could sit on the floor and read or write letters if we liked. I went to all of them. It was a new kind of music for me and, though I always brought along a book to read and didn't realize I was listening to the music, I really was.

As an added inducement to get me to go to camp willingly, I was allowed to take horseback riding, even though it was extra. Ever since my Zane Grey period I had been wild to get up on a real live horse, and as soon as I did I knew that was where I belonged and I would never again mourn not having a bicycle. I had a big chestnut mare named Sally. I rode her three times a week all that summer and I loved her. She had a silver mane and tail and a nose as soft and smooth as a mushroom and eyes as deep and gentle as mountain pools. I think she loved me, too. Once Hank had pointed out how to hold the reins and what to do with my knees and toes and heels and elbows, there wasn't anything else she had to teach me, because Sally herself showed me exactly how to handle her. We understood each other. I loved everything about riding, not only the sense of power it gave me, and the close wordless communion between Sally and me, and the motion and speed, but also the special way of seeing places you rarely get any other way. The trails led through woods, through dark, leafy, damp-smelling places and sun-dappled ones, and then out onto a road in full sunlight, past farms and across wooden bridges over gurgling brooks or roaring gorges, and from your height on a horse you could see much more than if you had been merely walking.

When I first got to camp, I didn't know anyone. It was an all-girls' camp, and that first night in the dining room there were more girls gathered in one place than I had ever seen before. Furthermore, since there was a camp uniform, we were all wearing the same green and white garb. Because it was such a good camp, many of the girls came back year after year. It was easy to spot the repeats, because they bubbled over with the joy of seeing each other again and being back at dear old Camp Stowe. Those few whose first summer it was were even easier to pick out, since we all looked glum and apprehensive and didn't know the words to the songs all the others began singing lustily the minute we sat down to dinner. One of these, Eleanor Marx, an unsmiling, sharp-featured girl with shrewd eyes, whom I had already met since she was in my bunk, sat beside me. While I was observing that this camp, unlike any I had ever heard of, had regular waitresses, and that the food, which looked good, was brought to the table on platters and set before the counselor at the head of each table, who then served us, Eleanor leaned to ask me a question in a low, confidential tone.

"Do you smoke?" is what I thought I heard her say.

"Do I what?" I asked in my normal voice.

"Shhh!" she said. "Smoke."

"Smoke what?" I said.

"Cigarettes, dummy. Wha'd you think, salmon?"

I giggled. "I'm too young," I said.

"What do I look like? Your great-aunt?"

"You could be any age," I said. "You have that kind of face."

"I'll teach you how to smoke," she said. "I've got a pack of Luckies in the bottom of my trunk."

"Okay," I said.

"And let's french the counselor's bed."

"Okay," I said.

We stole off into the woods the following afternoon, armed with Eleanor's Luckies and some other equipment she deemed

138

necessary for furtive smoking: peppermints to sweeten our breath should anyone chance to kiss us afterwards, and Band-Aids to secure our index and middle fingers against telltale nicotine stains. However, once we had gotten deep into the woods and settled in a safe spot with our fingers bandaged, we discovered that the matchbook Eleanor had brought contained only three matches, and as there was a breeze and we were inexperienced, we never did get one of the cigarettes lit. It was too late to try again, but we did french Hank's bed that night and the next. She never said a word about it, but on the fourth morning we were told that we had been invited to sleep that night in Auntie (pronounced in the English way) Beck's bunk. Although I was to spend five summers at Camp Stowe, I never discovered what Auntie Beck's position was, but it must have been administrative, as she had nothing at all to do with the campers. She was a straight-backed, elderly woman, not much more than four feet high and splinter-thin, with a severe, sharply lined face and eyes as small and black and cold as a bird's. She appeared at most meals and functions, but at other times only rarely, usually striding across the campus as though it were a moor, invariably dressed in riding breeches and boots and a funny, narrow-brimmed felt hat that covered all of her head and her ears. She had a brown leather riding crop, one end of which was permanently wound around her right hand, while from time to time she snapped the whip end against the calf of her boot. She was an intimidating little woman.

Auntie Beck's bunk was in a secluded clearing in the woods, set apart from the rest of the camp. Clutching pajamas and toothbrushes, Eleanor and I approached it feeling very much as Hansel and Gretel might have felt had they had advance knowledge that the lady of the house was a witch. We were only too well aware that this invitation was a form of punishment, though no one had mentioned our crimes.

"They won't even be able to hear our screams," Eleanor said in a hoarse whisper. She was pale with fear, but I couldn't help suspecting that she was also thrilled. We had speculated all day on what Auntie Beck was going to do to us. Eleanor's imaginings ran to physical torture but my own guess was that we were in for a sharp tongue-lashing, which, coming from Auntie Beck, might be far more to be feared.

She opened the door to our timid knock as the bugle sounded taps off in the distance where our peers were settling in. It was the only time I was ever to see her with neither hat nor riding crop. She smiled a small, thin-lipped smile and said, "Come in, children. Welcome to my castle." It was a snug one-room cottage, all darkly varnished logs, with lots of books, a table in the center with a kerosene lamp already lit on it, a pair of cushioned rocking chairs, a primly made-up bed in one corner and, diagonally across from it, bunk beds in a curtained alcove.

"I guess we better go straight to bed," Eleanor suggested hopefully, her eyes darting nervously from the floor to Auntie Beck's face. "The bugle blew."

"Get your pajamas on," Auntie Beck said, "and then we'll sit down and have a little chat."

We bolted for the curtained alcove, Eleanor and I, and, shivering from the cold night coming on as well as from nervousness, we dawdled over undressing as long as we dared. When we were in our pajamas we neatly and painstakingly folded our clothes and laid them on the foot of the bottom bunk bed and then, with mathematical precision, lined up our four shoes under the bed. When there was nothing more we could think of to do, we stood for a moment regarding each other, while I wondered at the intimacy of our shared plight. I hardly knew Eleanor. I wasn't even sure if I liked her.

"You go first," Eleanor hissed, giving me a shove that sent me reeling through the curtains and nearly into Auntie Beck's lap. Auntie Beck, a book open before her, was seated at the table to which she had drawn up a third chair. She looked up at my abrupt entrance and I tried an embarrassed smile. She closed her book and smiled back. The light of the oil lamp softened her face and I saw that her smile, if not exactly kind, was genuine. She patted the chair beside her and I sat down in it and, glancing at her book, saw that it was something called *Sonnets from the Portuguese.* Eleanor appeared and slid into the third chair.

"I do covet my privacy," Auntie Beck said crisply, "but once in a while it's nice to have company." A plate of cookies and three glasses of milk had materialized on the table, and she passed these around. "I always like a little bedtime snack," she said. "I don't know why it isn't a regular part of camp policy. Help yourselves."

With the first sip of milk, my nervousness subsided and I began to be curious about Auntie Beck, about what kind of person she was and what her life was like. It was at this moment that she herself said, "Tell me a little something about yourselves, girls. Tell me about your lives. Eleanor?"

Eleanor looked up, startled. "My life?" she mumbled. "What about my life?"

"Do you like it? Are you happy?"

Eleanor stared at her and then burst into tears.

"Why are you crying?" Auntie Beck asked after a while.

"Because my mother has migraines," Eleanor sobbed. "She has them all the time. Ever since I was born."

Auntie Beck nodded at her.

"And insomnia," Eleanor added on a fresh wave of sobs. "She feels terrible all the time."

Eleanor blew her nose and stopped crying. "She's seen every kind of doctor there is," she said. "Nothing helps."

"Finish these up," Auntie Beck said, passing the cookies around again. "Would you like some more milk? What about you, Allegra? What about your life?"

I thought for a while. "It's a complicated question," I said.

"Life is complicated," Auntie Beck said.

"Yes. But maybe it will turn out all right. Is that a book of poetry?"

"Yes."

"Is it in Portuguese?"

"No, English. You may borrow it if you like." Then, apparently satisfied, Auntie Beck bustled us off to bed. No scolding, no lecture. I climbed into the top bunk bed and sank into a soft cloud. It must have been a feather mattress, because it folded itself about me like a warm embrace and I was instantly asleep.

"That was some punishment," Eleanor grumbled next morning as we headed away from Auntie Beck's cabin towards the dining hall and breakfast.

"This is a pretty good camp," I said, clutching Auntie Beck's book. "I may even end up liking it."

More than half the summer had gone by between then and the day I made public my crush on Hank, and, afterwards, reclining in my beech tree, I sat looking up at the sky through the glistening leaves. Clouds scudded by and between them the sky showed blue, that miracle-pure blue that comes after days of rain when you've almost forgotten blue. I had a lot to think about. The girls' horror at my use of the word love in connection with Hank had started me thinking. I'd forgotten that, except for a couple of men who worked on the grounds, we at Camp Stowe were all of the same sex. Not forgotten it so much as simply not thought about it. I tried to understand why. Without boys or men, except in group singing, the range and variety seemed pretty much what it was in the outside world. We had the doers and the dreamers, the leaders and followers, the tough and the gentle. I wondered if we were different because of the absence of men, different than we would have been with them, or whether it might be that we were in some way freer to be more ourselves. I was certainly beginning to feel better about myself than I did around my father and David and even my mother, who was so much my father's wife that, if not the disease itself, she was its carrier. It was as though I were growing a new personality, one that had nothing to do with whose daughter or sister I was. The tone was set by the directors and the counselors, women who took themselves seriously, and who took us seriously as well; we were looked upon as real people with real potentials, real futures, real problems. They were the first group of women I knew who *did* things, things other than bridge and golf and shopping and hiring houseworkers. These women painted, played music, sang, acted, danced, taught, read. One was a theatrical director; another a botanist; a third, our camp physician, did medical research the other months of the year.

I wondered what kind of person my mother would have been in a setting like this. Although she hadn't gone to college, as the only thing she was expected to do was to make a good marriage, she had been the smartest and most popular girl in her graduating class in high school, and I knew she was intelligent, because she was a wizard at word games and puzzles. I couldn't help feeling sorry for her. It had simply never occurred to her, having married a successful businessman, as had most of her friends, to do anything with her own life.

So it was something of a surprise to me to come upon this new kind of women, women who were doing interesting and maybe even valuable work, doing what they loved and found exciting. Most of the campers were from families similar to mine, so I was sure they must all have been made as hopeful as I by all these proofs that our horizons might not after all be so limited. But not at all.

"They're still pretty young, remember," Naomi Albrecht pointed out. "In their twenties. How much do you want to bet that in the next five years they'll be married and have babies and have forgotten all about their careers."

"Not Dr. Allison," I said. "Not Hank. Not Aitch or Judson."

"The ones who don't get married will just become dried-up old maids. Who wants to be one of them?"

The scorn in her voice was nothing new to me. I had been hearing it all my life in connection with old maids or spinsters. As far as I could see, there was nothing more shameful to a girl than not to have her hand chosen (or to surrender it) in marriage. It meant that you weren't good enough, or that you were unnatural; in either case you were a failure.

"Why do they have to be 'dried-up' old maids?" I said. "They all seem pretty attractive to me."

"*Now,*" Naomi said. "While they have their youth."

I thought of a conversation I had had that spring with my cousin Sonia. As a rule I avoided conversations with her, but I'd gotten trapped into this one by having carelessly let fall the information that instead of marrying when the time came, I thought I might have a series of interesting affairs.

"You'll never be really happy as a woman," Sonia said, "until you have your own sweet baby at your breast."

I recognized this as something her mother, my Aunt Gertrude, was always saying to her, but I refrained from throwing up.

"What a disgusting notion," I said. "You mean, because of being female nothing else will ever make *you* happy?"

"Not really happy. Not in the same way."

"How about if you became the world's most famous tap dancer and a Hollywood star and got to do love scenes with Robert Taylor and Tyrone Power and never had another pimple and could eat all the candy you wanted?" I said, cruelly playing on all her weaknesses.

"That would be nice, too," she admitted. "But I could do both."

"And what's so great about nursing a baby?" I said. "You feed it and then you have to hold it up and burp it and then it falls asleep and wets its diaper and you have to change it and then it wakes up and cries because it's hungry again. All you're doing is keeping the machinery going until it can run itself."

"You're just not normal," Sonia said, shaking her head sadly. "There's no point even talking to you."

In the social hall, not far from my tree, I could hear the quartet practicing. It made me feel good to know that Hank was near and to have the sound of her violin drift up into my treetop. I thought about love, about different kinds of love. I was pretty sure that in spite of everything I loved my mother and David and Grandma. It was even possible that I loved my father. Still, wasn't that because they had always been there and were so familiar? But what was a crush? I had done enough reading to know about passion, and even lust, and I wondered if it was that that was beginning to grow in me. But it was too hard to think about. I wanted to feel whatever it was I was feeling without complicating and spoiling it with words.

I drifted back into a state I had been in so often that summer, a vague, restless, not entirely happy euphoria.

I was supposed to be at fencing, but as fencing and archery were my two worst activities, I avoided them as often as possible, although this was against the rules. I did have some free periods during the week, but not enough for all the thinking and reading I had to do that summer. Since the night in Auntie Beck's bunk I had been reading a lot of poetry. Although we had read some poems in school, I felt as though I had made a new discovery. The poems in school had been either too long and told stories, or too short and inspirational. They were not like the poems I was finding now, medium ones, like sonnets. They were more personal and seemed like a new kind of language to me: pure crystals formed out of ecstacy, or out of an equally unbearable agony, the pearl in the oyster, the butterfly bursting free of the cocoon and trembling in its first flight. Poems spoke to me in an entirely new way.

It came to me then, in the tree, that the finest thing I could do about my crush would be to write a poem to Hank. I began to struggle with it in my head, and then on paper during rest period. I had to stop for tennis and, after that, volleyball, but my mind continued to work on it. I skipped swimming that afternoon and escaped with my pad and pencil to the woods where I finally finished it. Here is the poem:

TO HANK

When first I did perceive you with my eye,
I saw you were a fair and comely maid.
And next I did perceive you through my ear
When Bach and Mozart in the Social Hall you played.
Lest eye and ear should not suffice, dear friend,
Know that it is my heart as well you now invade.

When I had polished it and copied it out in print, I read it through about ten times. Nothing I had ever done had been as satisfying, but how would it seem to Hank? I decided not to sign it, slipped it into an envelope, and a few minutes before the dinner bugle, I stole into the dining room and left it propped against Hank's water glass. When we filed in for dinner, I was already sorry about the whole thing because I was so nervous. What a stupid thing to have done. Now, of course, I had to compose myself into a picture of purest innocence and nonchalance, which I tried to accomplish by chattering away with Eleanor and never once looking in Hank's direction, though I was aware all the same of every move she made. It was as though instead of the two hundred and more souls in that big dining room, Hank and I were the only ones present. As soon as we had taken our seats after singing the predinner song to celebrate our gratitude for the joyous day that was drawing to a close and for the serene and gentle night that lay ahead, Hank reached for the envelope and opened it. Even though my heart was pounding so hard that I was sure everyone could hear it, I couldn't help stealing furtive glances at Hank's face while she read the poem. At first she looked surprised, and then just for a flash, amused, and then as I saw her eyes go up to the top of the page to read the poem again, her face showed nothing at all. When she had finished reading it for the second time she carefully refolded it, put it back in the envelope, and patted it into her sweater pocket. She looked over at Mitzi Swerdlow for about one second, and then she looked at me and smiled, a wonderful smile, and I knew it was all right.

After dinner, when we were walking back to the bunk, she took my arm.

"Thank you, Legg," she said. "That's a good poem."

"How did you know I wrote it?"

"I just did," she said, smiling.

Then we went on to have a conversation about whether I was going to write more poems, and whether I had a talent, and it turned into a literary discussion with no mention at all of the subject matter of my poem. I didn't realize this until later that night when I was falling asleep. The important thing seemed to be that I had written a poem, not what it was about. I wondered if Hank had been trying to save us both from embarrassment, and then I thought how clever she had been.

But I did go on writing poems, first on the theory that one good poem deserves another, and then because writing poems is like eating salted peanuts; there is no turning back. Most of my poems were about Hank, or about Restless Yearning, but some were about Death and Nature. That summer Nature was unusually important to me; my new feeling for it was connected to the way I felt about Hank and poetry and Tchaikovsky's *Pathétique,* and it was getting to be almost more than I could stand. Once, for absolutely no reason, I burst into tears watching the sun set across the lake while the swallows wheeled and dipped. Another time, the sun came out after a shower and made a rainbow and the air had such a softness and smelled so sweet and piney that it made me drunk and I had to run off into the woods, where I fell asleep for over an hour. And another night, during a candlelight recital, listening to Schubert and looking through the windows at the stars, I suddenly felt that I was going to explode and I had to go outside and run around the social hall about a dozen times before the feeling went away.

I knew there was something the matter with me, some kind of severe mental illness, but I couldn't talk to anyone about it because I wouldn't have known how to explain it. Writing poems helped. It was taking the feeling and putting it somewhere outside myself, making a neat, manageable package of it. I spent more and more time in my beech tree.

I was up there one day while the quartet was practicing, working on a difficult poem that I couldn't get right. The lake had had an unusual infestation of leeches that week and I was trying to use this as a metaphor for love: how, aware of the pitfalls, you go swimming anyway because you have to take your chances, and, sure enough, when you come out you find one or more of these strange, uninvited creatures attached to you. They're hard to get off, sometimes the only way is to burn them off, but even so they take a part of you with them, your very blood.

I was vaguely aware that someone had come along and sat down on the bench beneath me. I looked down and I could tell by the short, prematurely gray hair that it was Judson. I went back to my poem, then, wondering why I couldn't get it to work, and my mind wandered off. Maybe the trouble was with the leeches. Grandma had told me that in the olden days barbers used to keep leeches for medical purposes. If you were sick they "leeched" you. The leeches were supposed to draw the impurities out of your blood. But did they really separate out the impurities, or did they merely take whatever blood they happened to get? And why should barbers have qualified as doctors? Except for the scissors, what did one thing have to do with the other?

These were some of the thoughts my mind was wasting itself on while below me Judson stamped out one cigarette and immediately lit another. It was late afternoon, a quiet time, as most of the camp was down at the lake. In a little while they would all come trooping back up the hill to shower and dress for dinner. It must have been a free time for Judson, whose specialty was nature walks. She knew a lot about mushrooms and ferns and the Latin names for all the trees. Tall and lanky, with a swinging athletic walk, she was one of those whom, at summer's end, it would be jarring to see wearing a dress and lipstick. She had a thin, pale face with features so regular that they left her face almost blank.

The Brahms Piano Quartet came to an end for the third time and, as the players all reached the end at the same time and without any discussion, I knew the rehearsal was over. One by one they came out and strode off in different directions. I watched for Hank. She was the last to come out, and when she appeared, Judson jumped to her feet and waved to her. Hank came over and they both sat down, Hank carefully putting her violin case and music on the bench beside her. I was just beginning to think about making my presence known, or coming down out of the tree, when I saw them turn and smile at each other, and then I saw Judson's hand close over Hank's. Neither of them said a word.

They just sat that way until we heard voices coming up from the road to the lake. Hank withdrew her hand from Jud's and they both got up and walked off in the direction of the bunks.

I stayed in the tree for a while after that, thinking about Hank and Judson and how quiet they had been, and then I tore up the poem because it was a lousy idea and when I got to the dining hall dinner was half over.

Chapter 12

When the back doorbell rang that Saturday morning, I went to get it, as I was nearest. It was the dry cleaner with two of my father's suits.

"Wait," I said. "I'll see if there's anything for you to take back."

I went to the head of the basement stairs and called down to Olga, "Is there anything for the cleaner?" There wasn't.

"No, nothing," I said to the delivery boy. He looked vaguely familiar, a tall, thin boy with straight black hair and some kind of foreign accent. I was about to close the door because I believed we had concluded our transaction when he smiled and said, "You are the sister to David Goldman?"

"Yes," I said.

"David and I were together in class last year," he said, "but since the graduation we are in two different high schools. I would like to greet him if he is at home."

It was pretty cold outside and he was wearing only a thin

jacket and looked slightly blue around the lips, so I told him to come inside while I went to get David, who was finishing his breakfast, reading the Rice Krispies box while he gagged on his milk.

"There's someone at the back door who wants to see you," I said.

"Who?" David said, surprised, since he never had callers.

"The dry cleaner. The delivery boy."

"Oh, him," David said, getting up. I followed him back to the pantry.

"Hello, Josef," he said.

"Hello, David," the boy said, smiling. He had nice teeth. "I was wondering how you are getting on in high school. Do you like Erasmus?"

"It's okay," David said. "How's Madison?"

"Terrible," Josef said, laughing. He looked at me and shrugged. "So crowded."

"Yeah, Erasmus, too," David said, and then they both stood there not saying anything, exhausted by this scintillating exchange, while I worried about David not asking him to come in out of the pantry.

"Well, perhaps I could come around some time when I am finishing working and we could have a conversation," Josef said. "Compare notes, as they say."

"Yeah, okay," David mumbled.

"How would it be this afternoon? I will be finishing with the deliveries about three o'clock."

"This afternoon I have a lot of work to do," David said. "Maybe some other time."

"What kind of work?" I said to David a few minutes later when the door had closed behind Josef. "How many friends have you got, for God's sake?"

"I have a recital coming up. Remember?"

"The recital isn't for another two months."

"I've got three long pieces to perfect. Besides, I don't know what he suddenly wants to see me for. We never had anything to do with each other in school last year."

"Maybe he was too shy last year," I said. "Wasn't that his first year in P.S. 193?"

"Yeah, they'd just come from Rumania. His father is the tailor who sits in the store window with the sewing machine."

"So what?" I said, conjuring up the image of Josef's father, a short, frail man with a beard and a yarmulka and the most closed, expressionless face I had ever seen on anyone. "So what if his father is a tailor?" Because of Melanie, I was much further along democratically than David, whose prejudices and values sometimes tended to echo our father's, infuriating me.

"So nothing," he said. "We just don't have anything in common."

"You don't have anything in common with anyone," I said.

"I just haven't anything to say to him. He wasn't even especially smart in school, except in math."

"How smart do you think *you'd* be your first year in a school in Rumania?" I said. "You have to give people a chance. For all you know, he's very musical. I bet he plays the violin. Don't most Rumanians play the violin?"

"You're thinking of gypsies," he said. "Anyhow, he's mainly interested in girls. Last year all the girls had crushes on him. They thought he looked like Errol Flynn.

"Errol Flynn?" I said, trying to imagine how they could have found any resemblance between that pale, thin boy and the debonair swashbuckling hero. The hair? The eyebrows?

"Furthermore, I'm sure he only wanted to come here to see

you," David said. "Last spring he asked me about you a couple of times."

"He *did?*"

"He wanted to know how old you were and things like that. Once he asked me if I thought you'd go to the movies with him some Saturday afternoon."

"He *did?*"

"I told him you didn't go out with boys yet. I told him you spent all your Saturday afternoons with your friend Melanie."

"You *did?*" I said, exasperated. "How come you never once mentioned anything about it?"

But that's the way David was, secretive. It was hopeless. I went upstairs to my room to examine my feelings and in a little while I discovered that I liked having a secret admirer. I looked in the mirror, trying to imagine what Josef could have found to admire in me, as so far it could only have been something he saw. But as usual the mirror didn't give me back a clue.

When I got downstairs again Mr. Hobie, one of Grandma's poker friends, was sitting in the breakfast room drinking coffee. As he was all alone there, I sat down to keep him company.

"Tell me about your life, Mr. Hobie," I said. I liked Mr. Hobie. He was a short, squarely built man with thick white hair and black eyebrows that beetled over the mildest of blue eyes, and he always dressed elegantly.

"I have had an interesting life and I regret nothing," he said. "I built the first Turkish bath on Manhattan Island. I have built dozens of six-story brick apartment houses in Brooklyn and Queens, as well as three large private home developments on Long Island. I started with nothing, not even an education."

"How *did* you get started?" I asked.

"You wouldn't believe it, but I will tell you anyway. When I first came to New York from the old country, fourteen years of age, I met a Scandinavian fellow who had invented a match you could not put out except by stepping on it or plunging it in water. 'You make those matches,' I said to him, 'and I will sell every one you can make.' And then I figured out who would need such matches: people out of doors in windy places. And so I rented a horse and went all along the Long Island shore selling the matches to fishermen, and soon I had my own horse and wagon and I sold other things as well. After about a year, some man from a big match company came up to me and said, 'I will give you five thousand dollars for the rights to that match.' In those days, five thousand dollars was a fortune. I went to my Scandinavian friend and I said, 'Will you take two-thousand five hundred dollars for the rights to the matches?' and he agreed at once, since the trade he had learned in the old country was carpentry and house building. And so together we went into the construction business."

"What happened to those matches?" I said. "I've never heard of matches that don't blow out."

"From that day to this, I never saw one again or heard another thing about them."

"That's really interesting," I said. "Tell me about Russia."

"In Russia we were very poor," Mr. Hobie said. "I had two older sisters and when I was six years old there were already two younger children, a boy and another girl, and my parents could not afford to keep me. They sent me to a miller some distance from my home, where I worked, helping to make the flour in exchange for my living. I loved my mother very much and so for a long time I was sad and felt as though my heart was broken. At night I used to sleep in a kind of loft on top of the mill. There was a big window and I would lay there looking out at the stars and I would think how big the universe is and what does it matter that one little six-year-old boy cannot stay with his mother because she is too poor. I came to love the stars. I wanted to learn everything there was to know about them. And that is how I came, years later, to whatever education I have. I have read every word of The Book of Knowledge from cover to cover, starting with A and ending with Z. I know many facts."

At this point, Grandma appeared at the breakfast-room door. She was all dressed up. She even had on a new hat with three cherries on the side and a little black veil that came down over her eyes to the bridge of her nose.

"Well, Mr. Facts," she said. "I am ready."

Mr. Hobie grinned at Grandma and got slowly to his feet. "She inquired about my life," he said sheepishly, "and so I was telling her about my life."

"Did you ever see your mother again?" I asked.

"Once. When I was leaving for America I went to say good-bye. I told her that when I had made my fortune I would send for the whole family to come to America. But by the time I was sixteen and had enough money, she was already dead."

"It's getting late, Mr. Moneybags," Grandma said, her eyes shining behind the veil. "The curtain arises in forty-five minutes."

"My Chrysler automobile will bring us to Radio City Music Hall in plenty of time for the rising of the curtain," Mr. Hobie said, gallantly convoying Grandma out. "Wait until you see it. A regular Versailles. My one regret in life is that I didn't build it."

Grandma was a movie buff, so much of one that she gave up the more respectable Midwood Theater for the Glenwood, a squalid, dirty little cave frequented by noisy kids playing hookey from school, when she discovered that the Glenwood, for even less money, gave her not two but three full-length features, plus selected short subjects. She spent many an afternoon there happily lost in other people's dreams. Sometimes she went at night because, in addition, there was bingo. If she had been to the Glenwood in the afternoon, we were served at dinner in amazing and relentless detail with her version of the plots of all three feature films. Once in a while I went with her to the Glenwood, but even so I had to hear the reprise. This wasn't as boring as you'd think, because what Grandma had seen usually bore little relation to what I had seen. It was often some peripheral detail buried in a subplot that loomed largest for Grandma. For example:

"Is coming to the new country a boat filled with ladies for the men to get married to because they are needing wives, so the ladies come off the boat onto the land and the men look them over to see which one they like, so then they go over to them and pinch their arms to see are they strong enough and will they be good workers, but one of the ladies, very young and especially pretty, they are all wanting and going over to her and telling her how big is their land and how rich they are, except one poor *shlemiel,* very skinny and sad is standing in the back not saying a word, just looking at her with big sad eyes, so she sees him and pushes through all the other men and goes over to him and says what about you, haven't you got something to say, so then he tells her he is poor and she says but you wouldn't always be, and then there comes on his face *such* a beautiful smile."

However, the night of her visit to Radio City Music Hall she never even mentioned the movie.

"Such a place," she said, her face still transfixed with won-

der. "Big enough and fancy enough even for the Pope. Drap-
eries so high they have to clean them with trolley cars. A
whole bunch of elevators to take you to the balconies. Everything gold and silver and marble and red velvet. The seats
more comfortable than in your own living room. Statues and
fountains, and even the ladies' toilet, I couldn't describe it to
you, the luxury. If they didn't show anything except one Krazy
Kat it would still be worth the price of admission. And then
the stage show! Don't ask. First a man playing a gold organ
the size of an elephant in the corner on the left, everything else
in darkness, and then when he is finished comes up out of the
floor like on an elevator an entire big symphony orchestra
playing classical music, and then in holes in the walls on the
sides, not even on the stage, lights are going on and there are
standing like statues ladies in beautiful long dresses, all different colors, holding burning candles, and then the curtain is
going up on a stage so big you could have an entire war on
it. But instead of a war comes out an army of girls all identical,
the Rockettes by name, don't ask me why, dancing their hearts
out, in a straight line, their pink legs kicking the exact same
height and the entire audience, including yours truly, screaming and clapping with pleasure."

We were just finishing dessert, and toward the close of this
recitation Olga came into the dining room and handed me an
envelope.

"It was under the back door," she whispered. She pointed
to my name on the envelope. "See. It's for you."

I should have had the sense to wait, but without thinking I
ripped open the envelope. Out slid a hideous big pink heart
with an arrow piercing it, drops of blood trickling from the
puncture. I turned it over and, on the back, printed in red
pencil, were these words:

Though it is not Valentine's Day
I think of you constantly
And that makes each and every day
Valentine's Day for me.
                  Guess Who.

I shoved the card back inside the envelope and thrust it onto my lap, and then I saw that everyone was looking at me, waiting for me to say something.

"Allegra has a boyfriend," David said.

"Who is it?" my mother said, looking pleased.

"It's Josef," David said.

"How do you know?" I said. "All it says is guess who. It's just some dopey card."

"Who's Josef?" my father said.

"The dry-cleaning boy," David said.

"Oh," my mother said, her expression changing to disinterested. "Some boyfriend!"

"You better pick someone richer than the dry-cleaning boy," my father said.

"I didn't pick him. He's not my boyfriend."

"Because once you're married, kiddo, you're off the payroll."

"It's just as easy to love a rich man as a poor man," my mother said.

"Married!" I screamed, getting up from the table and throwing my napkin down.

When I got home from school the next day, I discovered that there was blood all over my underwear. It took me a while even to realize that it was blood, and when I did I began to shake, because obviously I would be dead within the hour. That only lasted a second, because then I knew it was what I had been waiting for and dreading for about four and a half years. So I began to shake even harder. There it was, just like everyone said it would be, and I wasn't different from anyone else (female), and it was all out of my hands and fated. I didn't know if I was glad or if I would indeed have preferred to be dead within the hour.

My mother, naturally, wasn't home but Grandma was in the kitchen. When I had pulled myself together, more or less, I went down to her.

"I'm bleeding," I said.

She was chopping liver. She paused, the chopper suspended above the bowl.

"From where?" she said.

"Down there. From where ladies bleed from."

She buried the chopper carefully in the liver mush and took a step towards me and slapped my face. This surprised me. I burst into tears. Then she gave me a big hug and kissed me.

"What did you do that for?" I said. "Why did you hit me?"

"It's a custom."

"Oh, Christ," I said. "Those Jewish customs."

"*Mazeltov,* my darling."

"Thanks a lot. Where's my mother?"

"She's by Aunt Gertrude playing cards."

Aunt Gertrude's house was only a couple of blocks away. "Well, I guess I'll go tell her," I said. "She'd want to know."

Luckily, Sonia wasn't home. It was just the four ladies playing bridge in a smoke-filled room. I charged in and stood next to my mother's chair. Everyone looked up and said hello, but their minds weren't on it.

"I have to talk to you," I said to my mother.

"Wait till I'm dummy."

"What if you never get to be dummy?"

"Four spades," she said.

"It's pretty important," I said.

"In a minute. As soon as we finish this hand. You can sit down and wait for a *minute.*"

I looked at the gold sofa. I didn't know if the blood was still coming and if it was, where it was going.

"No I can't," I mumbled. So I stood on one foot for a while, and then I stood on the other foot, and then I stood on both feet, and then I took three pieces of Flora Mir candy out of the bonbon dish on the one corner of the bridge table that didn't have an ashtray on it. Then somebody finally took the last trick, but it wasn't over yet, as my mother had to argue with my Aunt Gertrude about some mistake she had made in the bidding, while at the same time Jennie and Ruth were yelling at each other about one of them having led the wrong card. Then everyone quieted down and my mother looked up at me and said, "Well, what is it, Allegra?"

"Can I see you in private, please?"

She sort of shrugged at the ladies and got up and followed me into the hall where she stopped.

"Not here," I said. "Come into the bathroom."

She followed me to the bathroom. I closed the door and locked it.

"I think my eggs have started to break," I said.

"Let me see."

I pulled down my pants and showed her.

"It's about time," she said with a big, happy smile, and then she, too, kissed me. You'd think I had actually done something!

"Well, darling, you're a woman now." She sounded sincerely proud of this. "Do you know what to do? The Kotex are on the shelf in the . . ."

"I know where they are."

"Well go home and put one on and change your pants."

"How do you put them on?" I said, beginning to feel really angry. "Do they just stick to you?"

"Oh, Lord! In my top drawer, on the lefthand side, you'll find a little pink belt with two safety pins attached to it. Grandma will show you how. I'll be home at five thirty."

"Grandma slapped my face."

She laughed. "It's an old Jewish custom."

I unlocked the bathroom door. "Some day," I said, "when you're not too busy and have a few minutes, you can tell me the significance of that particular charming Jewish custom. Though I can guess that it's got something to do with evil spirits and women being dirty."

As I walked down the hallway to the door I heard my mother say, "Congratulate me. My daughter's a woman."

"Sonia's been getting the curse a year already," Aunt Gertrude said in an airy tone of voice. "And she's two months younger."

"Sonia's more developed," my mother said. "Some girls develop earlier."

Developed!

"She's such a tomboy, I never thought it would happen to Allegra," my mother sighed. "Two diamonds."

"May they turn to salt," I muttered. "May they sit there eternally holding their cards among the smelly cigarette butts and the Flora Mir chocolates and may not one of them have an opening bid."

I slammed the door behind me, thinking about what boys were doing while girls, like negatives, like colds, were "developing."

162

"Okay," I shouted into the wind as I dawdled up Bedford Avenue. "Here comes the latest eggery."

Nothing would ever be the same again. Farewell, I murmured to my happy, carefree childhood.

Okay, biology, here comes another link in your crummy chain! Allegra Goldman, U.S.A., eggmaker, babymaker, female, woman.

Out of my hands. I would just have to make a stab at it. Woman.

Allegra.

Legg.

L'egg.

That's what had been hidden there all along, smack in the middle of that stupid name.

L'egg.

All egg.

Ra, ra, ra!

It was only a few nights after this, while my father was complaining at dinner about Franklin Delano Roosevelt, that Grandma said, "If I could interrupt for a minute, I have a short announcement to make."

This was so unusual, and her voice and her face were so grave that we all gave her our immediate attention. I saw, however, that her eyes were alive with excitement.

"Mr. Hobie has asked me to be his bride," she said. "So if nobody has any objections, wedding bells will soon be ding-a-linging."

There was a stunned silence. At least, there was a silence during which *I* was stunned. Grandma? Married? An old lady in her sixties? Why?

My father was the first to react.

"Where will you live?" he said.

"What do you mean, where will we live? Where do people live?"

"Well, I mean you live here and Hobie lives with one of his daughters, doesn't he?"

"So does that mean forever? Don't worry, we aren't going to move in here with you. Mr. Hobie owns buildings. In those buildings are apartments."

My mother jumped up then and ran around the table to Grandma, and they fell into each other's arms. "Oh, Mamma," she said, "I'm so happy." And to prove it they both burst into tears.

"I like Mr. Hobie," my father conceded.

Later, when I had partly absorbed the news, I managed to corner Grandma alone.

"Are you really going to get married, Grandma?" I said.

"Would I joke about such a thing?"

"But at your age, Grandma?"

She laughed. "What then should I do at my age, crawl into the grave?"

"Do you love Mr. Hobie?" I asked.

"Love, shmove."

"You *don't* love him?"

"Listen, Allegra, you know Mr. Hobie?"

"Yes."

"You like Mr. Hobie?"

"Yes."

"He's not a bad-looking man?"

"No."

"He's not weak or sickly to look at. Or otherwise."

"No."

"Strong, in fact."

"Yes."

"Not a stupid man. Reads books. Has a pretty good vocabulary for foreign-born, not a college education?"

"Yes."

"And kind. Not a cruel man. Am I correct?"

"Yes."

"Also, a man in comfortable circumstances."

"Oh, Grandma, why do you have to say it that way?"

"What? You're objecting to my English? In comfortable circumstances is wrong? It's good enough for on the radio, for ladies and gentlemen in penthouses in the moving pictures."

"If you mean he has money, say he has money."

"I didn't count his money. Poverty-stricken he's not."

"Okay, go on."

"So, adding it all up together, why wouldn't I marry Mr. Hobie?"

"All I wanted to know is do you love him?"

"It's not good for a woman to live alone. Worse, yet, to depend on her children."

"Why? Your children used to depend on you."

"That was different. They were children."

"But what's so terrible about it if you're not depriving them of anything? I mean, we have lots of room in the house and Daddy makes plenty of money."

"It doesn't matter. It's a shameful thing, a parent having to depend on the children."

"I never heard of anything so ridiculous."

"Besides, a person should have their own life. Don't you think I want my own home? To be the boss in my own house? To go to the store and buy what I want? To cook what I want for dinner? To invite who and when I please? To pick out the color paint I want on the walls? Even to have my own arguments? Much as I love your mother and father, you think it's the easiest thing in the world to live in their house at my age? Always to have to say I beg your pardon, if you'll excuse me, I wonder if you'd be so kindly?"

By this time I was close to tears. "Oh, Grandma," I said. "I never thought. I always felt you belonged here, were a part of the family just like anyone else. I always thought you were happy."

"Happy? Who's talking about happy?" she said. She patted my head. "Don't cry, darling. Wherever I'll be, you'll come visit. I'll make kreplach special for you."

Grandma's face was a lamp that was almost always lit during her waking hours. If it didn't shine with humor, it shone with happiness; and if it wasn't shining with love, then it was shining with goodness. She was forever giving me lessons in Life and she was often critical and sometimes angry, but, though I was afraid of her anger, even that shone with purity, so that there was never a moment of Grandma that was untrustworthy. Everyone loved her. That there had been pain in her life with us, that she might have suffered at all, was more than I could bear. I ran upstairs to my room to write a poem. I thought for a long time about Grandma, about old people who lived on the fringes of other people's lives. The loneliness of it. It wasn't so bad for men, like Mr. Hobie, who had their work, who could look at apartment houses they had built, who drove cars and had money in the bank and could give their grandchildren checks on their birthdays. But it was different for women like Grandma who had never been anything but wives and who, when their husbands died, weren't anything at all except mothers of grown-ups, which wasn't much. Apparently it meant nothing to Grandma that she had her good and cheerful nature, that she could make the world's best kreplach, blintzes, gefillte fish, shnecken, kugel, potato latkes and borscht; that she could sew a gorgeous stitch, so gorgeous that it had gotten me into bad trouble at school.

"This was done on a machine," Mrs. Bell, the sewing teacher, proclaimed in doom tones after inspecting my homework, part of a seam of the graduation dress those of my sex were required to toil over all year. My rebellion had echoed an earlier injustice, with matching futility.

"Why," I had demanded to know, "aren't the boys required to make their own navy blue suits? Who will be the tailors of tomorrow?"

"Absolutely done on a machine," Mrs. Bell repeated.

"I swear to God it wasn't," I said.

"Don't you swear to God in this classroom."

"Look," I said, grabbing the hated garment from Mrs. Bell and opening it to the two inches of seam I had done with my own hand full of thumbs. "Look at that. Did you ever see anything worse?" The erratic stitches not only wandered and jumped, they were grimed and spotted with blood. *"This* is *my* handiwork. I got that far and was just going upstairs to jump out of a window when my Grandmother calmly took it from me and said, 'Here, I'll show you how.' And then she did the rest of that seam. She was trying to teach me. I'd been working for an hour and she did all that in about two minutes!"

"Well, you'll just have to rip out what your grandmother did and do it over yourself."

"Rip it out?" I said, trying to keep my voice below a scream. "Rip out those beautiful stitches?"

"Every last one of them."

"I'd rather die," I said. "My grandmother *gave* me those stitches. With love in her heart."

"I appreciate your sentiments," Mrs. Bell said, sighing, "but you miss the point."

"These dresses are hideous to begin with," I said in a fury. "But can you imagine how much worse this one will be if I have to put it together myself? It will fall apart right there in the auditorium before I ever get my hands on that diploma."

"Which only proves that I am right to insist," Mrs. Bell said coolly, retrieving the dress and beginning to rip the stitches out herself.

"Flunk me," I wailed. "I'd be *proud* to flunk sewing. I'll never make it through this vale of tears anyway."

In the end, I prevailed upon Grandma to prostitute her art and to finish the dress for me, a little at a time, with stitches that gradually improved from an approximation of my own to something considerably less than her best. She did it with good humor; in fact, she chuckled over her forgery all the while she was committing it.

I had to laugh, thinking about it, even though I was so sad and on the verge of writing a bitterly doleful poem. The poem, I felt, should be about how a woman's center should be not in her hearth but in her own heart.

And then I remembered a Saturday afternoon during the previous spring, one of those first lovely spring days, when Melanie and I had gone to see *Potemkin* (part of my political education) in one of the upper-Broadway movie houses. Walking from the subway, I noticed for the first time that there were benches in the traffic islands that ran down the spine of upper Broadway, and that there were a lot of elderly women, most of them carefully dressed, sitting on the benches. There were a few old men, too, and a sprinkling of shabby young unemployed Irishmen, victims of the Depression, some of them drunk. But mostly they were old women. A few of them talked to one another, but for the most part they were silent and solitary and hopeless-looking. That anyone would sit in the middle of Broadway at all just because there were benches there, and not even because they were waiting for a trolley, astonished and depressed me.

"Who are they?" I asked Melanie.

"Widows," she said. "This neighborhood is full of residential hotels and rooming houses."

"And they actually sit there?" I said, stupidly.

"They haven't anything else to do," Melanie said with bitterness, understanding and sharing my reaction as she almost always could be counted on to do. "They're superannuated."

Superannuated. For a while I was distracted by the sad new word whose meaning was instantly clear to me. Superannuated. Melanie explained that it was one of the crimes of our particular society, of which her list was already so long that it was hard to believe there was room for more.

But this one came back to me now with such force that I felt I had the beginning of my poem, my metaphor.

By the time I went to bed that night, I had the poem. It was this:

SHIPWRECKS

On upper-Broadway islands planted
To part the traffic waves, north from south,
Slat-benched the bleached old Yiddish widows
Croon among the indigenous pigeons,
Marooned beside, thighed by thighed,
Strong idle Irish toughs, eyes glazed
By drink or hopelessness, as theirs by age;
Strange beachmates, the superannuated and
The unemployed, castaways out for the sun,

Gasping the treacherous April air
Filling the days with emptiness
Killing the days between spring and death.

The poem had taken me a little way from Grandma, turned me back in on myself and then out again into the world, a complex, spiralling voyage that left me so tired I went to bed without even brushing my teeth. Later that week I took the poem to school and submitted it, with some trepidation, to Miss Aldercox, my English teacher.

"If you really wrote this poem, Allegra," was her judgment, "you would deserve the English medal. Without question. But of course you couldn't have written it."

My despair was so great that all I could do was sigh and think: What's the use! But this was quickly succeeded by a sense of elation such as I had rarely known. That may well have been the highest tribute one could hope to receive from P.S. 193.

"What did you expect?" Melanie said later. "They can't cope with anything but mediocrity. Anything real confuses them." She went on to explain, at length, the changes the system of education would have to undergo before those of us, at either extreme from the norm, could actually benefit from it. Then she read the poem again. "It's an awfully good poem," she said. "Especially for someone your age. It has imagery and poignancy and social irony. Send it in."

"Send it in to what?"

"To be published. Send it to *The Brooklyn Daily Eagle*. They sometimes publish poems on the editorial page."

A week later I had a letter from *The Eagle*. It said: "Dear Miss Goldman: Thank you for sending us your excellent poem, *Shipwrecks,* which we plan to publish sometime during the week of April 10th, and for which we enclose our check for $10. We would be glad to see any more of your work that you might care to submit. Sincerely yours, Arvin P. Shaffer, Assistant Feature Editor."

I was alone in the house and I didn't know what to do. I read the letter a few more times then I began to tremble all over. Then I sat down on the stoop and cried for a while, and then I came back into the house and called Melanie up.

"They bought it," I said. "They bought my poem."

"Naturally they bought it," she said. "It's a very good poem. Why are you crying?"

"I don't know. I think I'm scared."

After I hung up I went upstairs to think about why I was scared and why I was crying. I had written a poem out of my own mind. It was going to be printed in a place where a lot of people would read it, people I knew and strangers, too. It had been paid for. Ten dollars was almost as much money as Olga made in an entire week, not counting room and board. What did it mean?

It could only mean that I was a real person, after all. I am a real person, I said to myself. Even in the grown-up world.

"Here is my first dollar," I said to my father the minute he came in the door that night. I thrust the check at him.

"What? What do you mean?" he said, taking the check and studying it. "Ten dollars! *The Brooklyn Daily Eagle?* What have you been doing, delivering newspapers? Girls don't have paper routes."

"I'm not delivering newspapers," I said. "They bought a poem I wrote. It's going to be printed."

"They bought a poem?" he said, taking off his hat and coat. "What poem?"

"Some poem I wrote."

"You wrote it yourself?"

"Of course I wrote it myself."

He still had the check in his hand when he went into the bathroom to wash up for dinner. When he came out, he handed the check back to me and said, "Well, well." I could see my news had put him in a good mood. When we sat down to dinner, he and my mother and David all looked at me for a while as though they were trying to remember who I was and where I had come from. Grandma was out, having dinner with Mr. Hobie's family.

"How long did it take you to write it?" my father said when he had finished his soup.

"I don't know," I said. "A couple of hours, maybe."

"Ten dollars. That's pretty good," my father said.

"It only took me a second to snap that picture," David said, "And I got twenty-five dollars." When he was twelve David had won second prize in a *Junior Scholastic* photography contest with a picture of a pigeon.

"I'm proud of you both," my mother said. "My children are both talented."

"How long is it?" my father said.

"How long is what?"

"The poem."

"Don't you want to see the poem," I said, "Instead of taking all these measurements?"

"What do I know about poems?" my father said, helping himself to salmon steak and asparagus and mashed potatoes from the platter Olga was passing around. "I never read a poem in my life. Fish!"

"We have to have fish once in a while," my mother said. "We can't have meat every night."

"Just what I had for lunch," my father grumbled.

"How am I supposed to know what you have for lunch?"

"I always order the special," my father said. "That way I know it's fresh."

"I suppose next you'll be wanting me to call Louie's every day to find out what the special is," my mother said.

"All right, let's see the poem," my father said. Naturally, I had a copy of it in my pocket, along with the letter from the newspaper, so I took them both out and handed them to him. He read the letter first, then turned to the poem.

"You won't understand it," my mother said. She herself had read it twice. My father chewed slowly over it.

"You're right. I don't understand it," he said. "I couldn't even pronounce some of these words. Where'd you learn these words?"

"Books," I mumbled. "That's what they're full of."

"So what's it supposed to mean? A bunch of old ladies with bleached hair sitting around on benches crooning songs? What's it all about?"

"Nothing," I sighed. "Forget it."

"I suppose it must be good or they wouldn't have paid you ten dollars for it," my father said. "But you can't prove it by me. I don't know anything about poems."

"That's okay," I said magnanimously. "I guess I wouldn't know how to run a dress business." Which wasn't strictly true; I was pretty sure that if I put my mind to it I could learn how to run any kind of business.

"I'd like to keep this," he said, folding up one of the papers and shoving the other back across the table to me. "There are a couple of people I'd like to show it to."

I looked at the paper he had passed back to me and saw that it was the poem.

"The *letter?*" I said, watching him put it, folded, in his shirt pocket.

And then I sat for a while, swallowing the rest of my dinner and looking at my family. It was my turn to wonder who they were and where they had come from and how they had managed, with nothing but their good intentions, to make me feel so dismal.

Never mind, Allegra, I told myself, you're a person.

You're a person.

You're a person.

Afterword

Allegra Maud Goldman, a poignant, incisive, and often hysterically funny coming-of-age story, is a portrait of the artist as a
young girl. The charting of the growth of its memorable heroine—the exceedingly precocious and "headstrong" Allegra Maud
Goldman and her struggles with (self) identification and differen-
tiation, innocence and experience—situate this autobiographical
"fiction of development" squarely in the tradition of the female
Bildungsroman, if not in a variant of that tradition, the *Künstler-
roman.* As a retrospective account of the attempts of a sensitive
protagonist to learn the nature of the world, discover its meaning
and pattern, and acquire a philosophy of life and the art of living
it according to the limitations of one's gender, the female
Bildungsroman is a narrative of both apprenticeship and
awakening.[1] Belonging to this illustrious and beloved tradition
are a great many of the heavily autobiographical novels that have
helped to shape the sensibilities of countless female readers over
many generations, whether in the form of exemplary stories or
cautionary tales—among others, *Emma, Jane Eyre, The Mill on
the Floss, Little Women, The Awakening, Claudine at School,
The Well of Loneliness, Their Eyes Were Watching God, Brown*

175

Girl, Brownstones, The Bell Jar, and *Sula,* as well as the autobiographies *Memoirs of a Dutiful Daughter, Memories of a Catholic Girlhood, I Know Why the Caged Bird Sings, Woman Warrior,* and *Bronx Primitive.*[2]

Novels of formation or development, as they are sometimes called, not only recount the evolution of a personality over time, but are themselves commentaries on the relationship between gender and genre, since they enact structurally and thematically the tension between individual possibility and social constraint. For Western readers the trope of "self and society," like the ideology it reflects, is so familiar and taken for granted as to be almost invisible. For even as they provide an account of the formation of a particular personality and the progression of an individual life story—always in the context of what it means to be a social subject—*Bildungsromane* emplot cultural messages: they are the narratives, however various, a culture (or subculture or counterculture) tells about itself.

Paradigmatically, novels of development are structured like arcs: they reflect a model of development that privileges process over product. And although origins and ends—of both lives and narratives—conventionally frame this process, the focus of a *Bildungsroman* is usually directed at adolescence, that most crucial transitional period in human sexual, interpersonal, intellectual, and moral development. Thus these novels begin in a number of ways, sometimes with the young heroine's rather mystically constructed birth, but more commonly with the advent of her self-consciousness. And although they are narrated from the vantage point of the end—whether it be death or a culturally authorized threshold or culminating point of maturity or self-understanding—the narratives themselves often close "prematurely," in medias res, as it were, long before the heroine's destiny has had a chance to fully play itself out.

This is certainly the case with *Allegra Maud Goldman,* whose investigation into the mysteries of personal identity and psychosexual development is framed by an opening that mimics her feisty emergence from the womb ("It's a girl . . . What could they have been thinking, naming me Allegra? I entered screaming and I'll go out likewise" [p. 1]) and a conclusion that, with the onset of menstruation and the publication of her first poem, signals her entry into "personhood." In the intervening pages, the complex and often conflictual connection between being a person and being a female is fully explored in the ironic mode: "A girl was something else I was beginning to learn I might be stuck with, and it was not the best thing to be" (p. 6).

Allegra's coming-of-age story expands our vision and understanding of the American immigrant experience at the end of the previous century through the first third of this century by offering a significant variation on the theme. The familial/social context described by Konecky is precisely *not* that of the prototypical Eastern European immigrant Jewish family who, having escaped from the ghetto, persecution, and famine in Eastern Europe, struggles against poverty, overcrowding, culture shock, marginalization, and anti-Semitism, while striving to assimilate and make good on The American Dream for the next generation—although the "background material" provided strongly suggests that for her parents' generation that was generally the world they knew. Allegra's grandparents had come to America with the masses of poor and uneducated Russian Jews in the late nineteenth century, and some of their children, as described by Arthur Hertzberg in *The Jews in America,* "turned into dress manufacturers and movie moguls, and some of their children and grandchildren became writers and professors."[3] The successful Americanization of the Goldman family had already taken place by the time Allegra appeared on the scene. Enjoying the benefits (as well as the "burdens") of a thoroughly privileged, upper-class Brooklyn lifestyle in the 1930s, replete with black chauffeur and Norwegian cook, she suffers no physical deprivation, only the angst that derives from having received too many mixed messages.

What exactly is Allegra's cultural legacy? This question haunts Allegra; and she seems to get no satisfaction from her immediate surroundings. The clash of cultural values, alternating by generations, as is often the case in nouveau riche immigrant families, constitutes one of the major themes of the book. Indeed, the Old World, as represented by Allegra's borscht-making, multilingual grandmother, exceeds its initial function as mere poetic device and eventually becomes a kind of objective correlative—a symbol that corresponds to a private emotional state and makes possible genuine aesthetic expression. It is Allegra's sadness and outrage at seeing the "superannuated" Yiddish widows sitting on the benches in the middle of Broadway that moves her to write her first published poem, "Shipwrecks" (p. 169).

What is so refreshing about Allegra's particular sense of entitlement is that it is less a reflection of a life of material prosperity and well-being than a contestation of it. It is precisely her pluck and perspicacity that make her such a compelling character, such an incisive witness to the workings of her own consciousness and of those around her. Embarking on the interior journey that is this autobiographical project, she says to the reader: "I have a terrible memory. I never forget a thing" (p. 4). Her relentlessly phenomenologically-oriented intellligence and perverse sense of the comic converge when, watching her father savor two dozen clams on the half shell, she contemplates their "slimy, unevolved," vulnerable existence: "This business of life! This business of *being!*" (p. 5) When asked by her dance teacher to imitate a lovely butterfly, "free and joyous in the beautiful sunlit sky," she prostrates herself on the floor. She is imitating "a dead one in a glass case in the Museum of Natural History" (p. 6).

Her particular rejection of the Oedipal family romance (in which she should grow up to be a woman like her mother so that she can marry a man like her father) takes many different forms over the course of the book. At each and every turn, however, it involves a wrestling with the great human dilemma of free will versus determinism. After running away one early spring evening at the age of seven, she concludes, "I knew then that I couldn't escape. Not yet. I was doomed to that house, those parents, my brother, this street, this borough. They were my fate. They were who I was" (p. 45). And after playing out several alternative scenarios in her head, she elaborates an enabling strategy that all female readers of fiction will find familiar:

> There must be a way I could survive; there must be a way I could separate myself other than physically. I could read all the time. While I was reading I wasn't where I actually was, I was where it was in the book. I would read, I would be wary and I would grow up. (P. 45)

Female readers have traditionally looked to fiction in general, and as Rachel Brownstein testifies, to novels that center on heroines confronting a specifically female destiny in particular, as the space that "explores the connections between the inner self and its outward manifestations—between the personal and the social, the private and the public—by focussing on a woman complexly connected to others, who must depend, to distinguish herself, on the gender that delimits her life."[4] By this point in Allegra's own narrative, she has been pondering that destiny for a while. Already, on the first day of first grade when the teacher goes around the classroom asking the children to announce their names, addresses, and what they plan to be when they grow up, Allegra (who has told us before she never gives the same answer twice) says—some fifty years before Sandra Day O'Connor became a household word—"A Supreme Court justice" (p. 18).

But, fortunately, unlike many prepubescent heroines who walk a fine line between self-conscious and self-indulgent, Allegra does not ever get obnoxious or too cute for her own good, and she seems virtually immune to sentimentality. Because all of her experience is filtered through, mediated by a (psycho)analytically-informed adult consciousness, the ironic distance between the two voices—the adult-inflected and the perceiving child's—produces and sustains that tension between expectation and fulfillment that is the pervasive and characteristic mode of the book. Allegra, infused with retrospective wisdom about the life she hasn't lived yet, has psychic needs she attempts to express, literally and symbolically. In chapter 7, which is devoted to existential dread, the intersecting themes of puberty, religion, mortality, and writing figure as signs to be decoded by her family. Not only can they not read the signs, they don't even know there is a subtext; it is Allegra who must make the connections between the symptomology, the disease, and the hoped-for cure. The scene in which Allegra's mother discovers that she has been throwing up every night and attempts to find out why is set up to play off the reader's expectations against Allegra's; Allegra preempts these by incorporating the desired maternal script into her own. Thus the dialogue includes the lines not said as well as those that are—"Now was the time for her to say . . . " (p. 82)—but always from Allegra's authorial and directorial perspective. In their heart-to-heart conversation that does not deliver, Allegra links her nausea to an overwhelming fear of dying in the hope that her mother will reassure her that her affliction is universal and age-appropriate, and therefore transitory. When her mother does not respond accordingly, Allegra "desperately cueing her," says, "Isn't it something everyone goes through? Isn't it just an ordinary, natural, normal, common thing?" Her mother, "dooming" her, says, "Of course not. It's just your wild imagination" (p. 82).

The often incongruous double vision of the autobiographer, both child and adult, reader and writer, is reflected and refracted through both language and event. A particularly significant moment in the narrative, one that refers to a common motif in both fairy tales and women's fiction—the awakening of the heroine from a long sleep to a new stage in physical development or psychic consciousness—occurs in the same chapter. During her month-long convalescence from a three-day coma (later identified by her sophisticated friend Melanie as a "nervous breakdown" [p. 96]) when Allegra withdraws from the dissatisfactions of quotidien reality in general and family life in particular, she discovers "a whole new world" (p. 87) of literature and learns that reading is not merely an escape but a source of intellectual stimulation, a way to expand the limits of one's own horizons. Her list of things learned stresses her own metaphysical preoccupations, mirroring an evolving quest into how human beings construct meaning in a universe they have not created and over which, ultimately, they have little control. Intoxicated by the rich and diverse commentary on the human condition that books offer and empowered by her own ability to engage in intellectual discourse, Allegra self-consciously seeks to join the community of readers and writers to which she feels she truly belongs. The typewriter she has requested, first used to inscribe her recently elaborated personal religion, becomes her metonymical link to the world of textual production, and to her eventual vocation as writer.

Thus when Allegra concludes that "money [is] not the most important thing in the world" (p. 87), and that ideas might constitute a higher form of currency in a different economy, her challenge to her family's nouveau riche "materialistic rationalist" (p. 88) ethic and its suppression of spiritual and intellectual inquiry for its own sake have long-range implications. This message Allegra gets loud and clear from the patriarch of the Goldman family, an authoritarian, bourgeois, and very successful dress manufacturer who, in a Jewish variation of Weber's theory about the transmutation of Calvinism into capitalism, equates wealth with earthly grace (or at least intelligence). Mr. Goldman's classic response to having met someone with impressive scholarly credentials would be, "If she's so smart, why isn't she rich?" (p. 54). He has bought, as it were, the entire pragmatic package of the American work ethic wholesale.[5] The mythos of the "self-made man" runs rampant in this household; but it's a myth Allegra demystifies. She conjures up a "literal image of a hand and arm rising slowly from a doughy mass, the hand then reaching down into the mass, from which it proceeded, painstakingly, blindly, to sculpt itself, my father" (p. 39). She even challenges the concept itself. "If he had to make himself," she says, "why couldn't he have made himself nicer?" (p. 39). Proving the preferability of showing over telling as a narrative technique, the imperious and choleric Mr. Goldman is described through a number of illustrative examples from his own linguistic repertory in which "productive" and "enterprising" dominate. Even though Allegra makes attempts to understand him, to contextualize his experience, it is ultimately against her father's fiercely materialist values that she learns to define her own sense of personhood— right up to the last page of the book when she experiences the delicious pleasures of creative achievement and self-worth as ones that transcend money.

Mrs. Goldman, though amenable to parody, receives somewhat more complex treatment than her husband. When she isn't desperately attempting to defend her husband from Allegra's scathing commentary, she is playing mah-jong or performing such elevated domestic duties as buying her children underwear from Abraham & Strauss. She suffers from a "nervous stomach" and sees a newly-minted psychiatrist for her problem, one who practices "family therapy" by actually joining the family for dinner. It is David, however, her neurasthenic, obsessive-compulsive son, who practices the piano to the exclusion of almost everything else, who is the real object of observation. When Allegra questions the professional diagnosis of David's "inferiority complex" and attempts to identify his psychic distress, she not only shows resentment at all the misguided attention directed at her younger brother, but challenges the notion that he is someone who "has to grow up to take his place in the world" (p. 65), while she is not. Allegra realizes that her own anguished concerns about "finding herself" as they have manifested themselves in intimations of mortality and the mortifications of the flesh are of no real consequence, given the inexorable terms in which her female life has already been cast. "Oh, you. You'll grow up and marry some nice man and have children. David is a boy" (p. 65). However restricted a view of the possibilities of female fulfillment has been offered her, the full significance of her mother's articulation of gender difference qua human destiny will not be grasped until later in the narrative when Allegra acutally meets a group of women "who took themselves seriously . . . and were looked upon as real people with real potentials, real futures, real problems" (p. 143). Allegra's internally embattled position as the non-dutiful daughter waging war against social conformity/sexual inequality necessarily involves a rejection of the maternal legacy, because her parents' marriage uniquely symbolizes her mother's tragic compromise with life. As she so indictingly puts it, her mother "was so much [her] father's wife that, if not the disease itself, she was its carrier" (p. 143).

The disease metaphor has been a dominant one throughout the book. Whether it is a matter of being fitted for a new dress at her father's place of business, attending her brother's bar mitzvah, or enduring the rituals surrounding her grandfather's death, Allegra experiences extreme malaise—malaise in a world where "tradition" is the complacent, hypocritical mask behind which insipid or even malignant adults hide. Allegra's sense of "epistemological loneliness"[6] starts to take on epidemic proportions; thus the summer she spends at an all-girls camp in the Massachusetts Berkshires is a crucially formative one. This environment is radically other: a bucolic landscape offering Allegra for the first time in her life natural beauty, physical freedom, culture as a source of aesthetic and sensual pleasure, opportunities for genuine solitude, and a harmonious women's community. Release from the oppressive strictures of family life and traditional expectations allows Allegra to envision other modes of experience, imagine romantic love through her first crush on a female counselor, and explore the means to express her desire. The mordant irony that has pervaded much of Allegra's narrative until now dissipates as she begins to discover the relationship between identity and alterity and the complexity of difference—all within the context of a virtually exclusive female environment.

> Without boys or men . . . the range and variety seemed pretty much what it was in the outside world. We had the doers and the dreamers, the leaders and the followers, the tough and the gentle. I wondered if we were different because of the absence of men, different than we would have been with them, or whether it might be that we were in some way freer to be more ourselves. (P. 143)

That in this environment young women were perceived to be "real people with real potentials, real futures, real problems" (p. 143) was positively revelatory for Allegra. The beech tree, her private retreat, becomes a symbol of that space where Allegra gathers her generous internal resources and learns affirmative strategies for coping with her dreams and frustrations, as she actively seeks alternative models of female behavior through friends and poetry. It is suggested that women and writing are destined to be an inextricable part of Allegra's life, as this book is of course testimony.

The camp chapter strikes the reader as anomalous because it seems so earnest; it lacks Allegra's characteristic critical edge, as if the autobiographer were once again awash in the "not entirely happy euphoria" of that particular summer and doesn't want to tamper with the idealized memory. Symbolically, of course, and in terms of the *Bildungsroman's* plot development—which focusses on the process of self-realization—what transpires in this chapter forms the climax of this narrative. Indeed, its tone and style are so radically different from the rest of the narrative that the final chapter, which recounts Allegra's return to family life, seems "merely" the necessary postscript, but here it is precisely the emplotment of the "necessary" that makes it interesting. In other words, Allegra may have changed over the summer, but home life most certainly did not: that disjunction Allegra realizes with bitter and poignant clarity. Her almost simultaneous accession to sexual maturity and literary success, and her family's mystifying reactions to both events, externalize and corroborate her forging identity as a woman who writes and who is read by others; but what she also *still* sees through her family's eyes is a distorted reflection of herself. This profound misrecognition, however, has no corrosive effects; instead it creates a new self-awareness. What was background becomes foreground and vice versa, as the changed Allegra sees herself differently, but only because she has another context in which to envision another Allegra. The technique or strategy of defamiliarization—estrangement from the familiar—is a prerequisite for aesthetic perception and production. Whether that reframing is chosen or imposed, seeing the old in a new context is what makes art possible. The challenge to Allegra's own preconceptions about herself crystallizes the ending whose point is to mark the completion of a phase of her life and chart new directions for the next. Allegra is on her way to becoming the kind of woman she would respect—"a real person"—but she might not have known this if she hadn't received the kind of validation of self-projection and invention that sometimes only the outside world can provide.

Allegra's style, voice, time, place, and family are essentially, Edith Konecky says, her own, even if the young heroine's "feminist consciousness was more articulate and precocious" than Konecky's could have been "back then."[7] Like most women of her generation, Konecky's passage from being a writer by vocation to being one by profession was gradual and not ongoing. At the age when Allegra was writing poetry, Konecky was writing "short stories and novels, mostly Westerns," though it was long after New York University and Columbia University and twenty years as a suburban wife and mother that she started writing *Allegra Maud Goldman* at the MacDowell Colony. She says that she was very happy there. One can't help but draw parallels between Allegra's catalytic experience as a summer camper and Konecky's at the writers' colony. (Perhaps there, like Allegra, she had a favorite beech tree.) Recently, she published another autobiographical coming-of-age novel, *A Place at the Table* (1989), about a spunky and talented, financially secure woman in her late fifties struggling with the demands of writing, love, and the body. Konecky concedes that Rachel Levin "must be Allegra grown up." In addition to some short fiction and poetry, she has two as yet unpublished novels as well, one that "covers much of the middle ground between *Allegra Maud Goldman* and *A Place at the Table*," the other "as unautobiographical as [she] could make it." Fortunately for her readers, Konecky's predisposition toward autobiographical expression is also her forte. But in *Allegra Maud Goldman* she has not only drawn on her own sensibility and experience to create a character who joins the ranks of other supremely spirited and intelligent literary heroines, she has provided a view of a culture quite satisfied with itself and blissfully ignorant of the outside world. For of the many messages one can take away from *Allegra Maud Goldman,* some of the most resonant and powerful remain implicit throughout the text: its resolutely microcosmic perspective only accentuates its larger historical context, the absence of historical referents in fact calls greater attention to them. At the narrative's close the reader knows along with the adult narrator that Allegra's life, brimming over with singular potential, cannot fulfill itself in the terms in which it is initially cast—not for lack of desire, will, or means certainly, but because World War II looms on the horizon. The interlude enjoyed by Allegra's privileged milieu will soon be over. As *Allegra Maud Goldman* approaches its end and celebrates all that is represented by a life poised between childhood and personhood, the becoming of a woman of promise is ironically set against a world in rapid and horrific decline. Thus the aesthetic and social values expressed in Allegra's poem "Shipwrecks" must be strong enough to resist both the relatively benign ignorance of her immediate surroundings and the malicious intent of the larger world. Otherwise, Allegra, however vigilant, will not develop further, she will not survive intact, and neither will the culture she has learned to hold dear.

Bella Brodzki

Notes

1. For a fuller elaboration of this theme in the female *Bildungsroman* tradition, see the introduction in *The Voyage In: Fictions of Female Development,* eds. Elizabeth Abel, Marianne Hirsch, and Elizabeth Langland (Hanover, N.H.: University Press of New England, 1983) and Susan Rosowski, "The Novel of Awakening," 49–68, above volume. See also Marianne Hirsch, "The Novel of Formation as Genre: Between Great Expectations and Lost Illusions," *Genre* 12 (Fall 1979), 293–311.

2. For a more extensive discussion of the preeminent place reading holds in the minds and hearts of women and its relation to the formation of a feminist consciousness, see Rachel Brownstein, *Becoming a Heroine: Reading about Women in Novels* (New York: Viking Press, 1982). For an examination of the role of the texts in which the characters are readers see *Gender and Reading: Essays on Readers, Texts, and Contexts,* ed. Elizabeth Flynn and Patrochinio Schweickart (Baltimore: Johns Hopkins University Press, 1986) and Carla Peterson *The Determined Reader: Gender and Culture in the Novel from Napoleon to Victoria* (New Brunswick: Rutgers University Press, 1987).

3. Arthur Hertzberg, *The Jews in America* (New York: Simon & Schuster, 1989), 162.

4. Brownstein, xix.

5. I am grateful to Joyce Freedman-Apsel for her insight on this point in fine, but also for her general attention to the Goldmans' social and historical situation.

6. Michael Chandler, "Adolescence, Egocentrism, and Epistemological Loneliness" in *Language and Operational Thought.* Topics in Cognitive Development, vol. II, ed. Barbara Presseisen, et al. (New York: Plenum Press, 1978), 137–45. Chandler characterizes epistemological loneliness

as the adolescent's existentialist response to increasing awareness of her/his own subjectivity, i.e. radical isolation in the world. I would like to thank Barbara Schecter for introducing me to this concept in developmental psychology.

7. All quotes from the author are taken from a letter written to me on January 22, 1990.